The Zombie Billionaire

P. J. Hafner

Birchbark Publishing

The Zombie Billionaire / P. J. Hafner

ISBN-13: 978-0692562253

He who endures, conquers.

- Persius

1

Name's Trick Chasseur, and I'm lucky to be alive. Maybe.

I was thinking that same thought not long ago, just as the door to our temporary hideout was giving way. I knew that within a few moments, I'd have to see if that luck thing had changed. Figured the door's lock would probably go first, but the hinges also looked ready to snap.

The hideout we were in appeared to have been someone's toolshed or garage at one time. A no-nonsense cellar built on a small hillside, half underground, the door opening to what used to be their yard. Nice and dark and cool in the summer heat – that was good. But ancient, clammy, smelly, and musty. Not so good. Full of mildew and deterioration.

That deterioration included the door and its hardware.

"Remember. Head shots only!" Margo said. More instructions we didn't need, summoning authority she didn't have. But it was no time to argue.

Ruby looked at her with a mix of irritation and fear, then glanced at me for assurance. I summoned some confidence and gave Ruby my best smirk of a smile, one I know she'd come to like. She tried to smile back. But with the moans outside the door and the barrier rattling with each push from the freaks on the other side of it, the terror crossing over Ruby's face won over. Nothing I could do to help. Except, of course, to kill what was causing the fear.

I planned to. I looked in Ruby's eyes for another

second, then set my backpack down to my left, my canvas satchel to the right, and switched my gaze back to the cellar door, shotgun in hand.

Quick break: before we start shooting, I'll fill you in regarding my partners. Ruby – dark-haired, curvy and beautiful – was basically a sweetheart; Margo – blonde, slim, almost beautiful – was basically a bitch. But at the time they were both angels as far as I was concerned. The two women were my companions and my friends, as well as my lovers.

And even better: they were both armed.

Margo on my left held a 20-gauge pump shotgun, and Ruby on my right held a lever action .30-30 rifle. I was between them with my own shotgun, a 12-gauge side-by-side double barrel, completing a nice little defensive semicircle, just twitching with ammunition. I had two eager rounds in my gun – the max of course with a double barrel – and eleven extra on the gun's attached ammo belt. Margo had four in her gun, but she had a good six or so in her own reserve supply. Ruby had four bullets left to her name, now all in the rifle.

"Stay frosty, people," whined Margo. More orders. *Just shut up and get ready to shoot, you nag.*

By the way, I *thought* that last part, the *nag* comment, instead of saying it. Remember that little detail about her being my lover? That definitely bought her a little wiggle room with insubordination. Just so it didn't go too far.

Two seconds after Margo's annoying comment – her most recent one, that is – the hinges on the hideout's door warped just a little further. A grey-blue hand pushed through a new opening near the top hinge. Another similar hand, this one decayed even more than the first hand, and a sick whitish grey in appearance, felt under the door, pushing aside the ancient dirt there that had created the seal in this old cellar. Two more thumps from some other thing out there crashing into it, and the ancient door flopped down to the earthen floor with a thud.

And seven zombies lurched toward us.

Seven of them, only three of us. But we had guns, and between us 27 rounds ready to pop. The zombies had none. And what's more, *I* was there. Generally, that counts for a lot.

At that moment, I focused on their filthy talons reaching out toward us, their mouths agape in anticipation of the bite. Two of the freaks groaning, one growling, the other four soundless in hungry yearning as they ambled ahead. With predictable results, we directed our weapons their way.

Ruby and Margo awaited the green light, and I kept my command simple like usual.

Here's something to groan about, goon squad.

"Now."

In the tight quarters of the cellar, the bursts and thunder of our gun blasts exploded the senses: sight, hearing, feeling. Smoke plumed ahead in a thin cloud. The muzzles of our firearms belched sparks and pink-orange flames to match the booms. Churning, flailing zombie bodies met the punishment, their forms punched back and down with the explosive gun shots. The attackers were defenseless against the blasts.

Justifiable homicide. But not heroic. Awful, really. No normal person enjoys doing something like that. But it was either administer and endure the fireworks which tore apart our adversaries – who were once human, like us, but now monstrosities – or feel those foam-covered fangs gnawing into us. Their disgusting, dirty nails digging into our skin as they did it. Not a hard choice. Thank goodness for guns.

I had thumped the nearest two geeks first, then

Margo whacked the next closest. Ruby took the fourth one out with her lever action rifle, using two of the last four .30-30 bullets she had left. She first made a non-vital shoulder shot, blowing the monster's right arm off, then a good skull shot. One wasted bullet, then a deliberate, surefire rifle thump – *pow, pow* – resulting in that undead character instantly down and vanquished. And finally quite dead.

Damn. Pretty serious damage. Just like any other time a zombie's head is burst with a deer rifle. Extreme result…too much really. So much so that a person would definitely want to be back a ways when making that kind of bullet placement with a high-powered rifle. Don't want any of that zombie blood misting over you, just in case.

Sickening scene or no, Ruby had aced the thing as soon as there'd been a clear shot, not waiting for it to get closer or become more exposed for the execution. Like I'd told her in the past, always take the first shot that presents itself. Don't wait until you can "see the whites of their eyes" or some such, because it might not end well. Nice execution on that particular zombie reject; Ruby hadn't been born a warrior, but she'd been improving steadily.

Margo did as expected. She might have been a nag, but her hand-eye coordination for shooting was stellar, and she made no apologies when killing to save her own life. Nor when saving Ruby's or mine.

Like most showdowns, this one was brief. An actual shootout – or an ambush in this case – often goes down many times faster than they used to show in Hollywood productions years ago. The movies often displayed aiming, ducking, darting, missing, reloading and gunfire exchanges for an entire minute or more. In reality, like this time, the shooting is usually over in seconds. So fast you're left wondering what exactly happened. I'd estimate this particular hammering of zombies took nine seconds, tops.

Oh yeah, taking out those remaining zombies. Next two: I popped them in the back of the head with my two reloaded barrels as they retreated, the creatures seeming unsure of themselves, their animated bodies disoriented and slow. Each zombie head nearly disintegrated upon the blast from the double barrel I've come to love. I just pointed and took easy shots at the clueless ramblers. Real fair, huh? Maybe you don't think so. But I say f –…uh, well, the heck with it. Take 'em out when you have the chance. Or it could be you next.

Six of the seven mutants that attacked us that day went down in the described barrages. The seventh somehow ambled and stumbled back outside, out of the cellar and into the greenery and light. It's pretty atypical for any zombie to retreat – we just had three of them do it – but you see it once in awhile.

So, at that point in this particular run-in, there was one threat left to subdue. One lurching zombie, a member of the hungry but losing team, now fleeing.

Concerning the last staggering zombie, and its necessary execution, a change-up was in order. Shooting was the optimal method to dispose of them, but exceptions occurred. Had to save our resources. This was a situation in which to forget about shooting for the time being; instead, kill the thing without wasting ammunition. It was time to use a quieter approach. What other safe way is there to kill the walking dead, besides using a loaded gun?

Well, one way is to put a patented Trick Chasseur maneuver into play. Just what exact maneuver might that be, you may ask. Watch and learn.

I reached for the soft-sided canvas case I'd set on the

ground moments earlier, right before we blasted the rejects. The four-foot long case is an item I carry with me at all times; usually I keep it strapped across my back. Along with some miscellaneous accessories, one main weapon resided in that canvas case.

And what a weapon: my pole pruner. A pole pruner? You, the reader, may wonder about this, not sure how a tool formerly used by landscapers and homeowners to trim out-of-reach branches would make much of a weapon.

Good question. Here's how.

The classic pole pruner, back in the days of the manufacturing of hardware store products, was often made of three telescoping tubes, each three feet long. Once all three sections were extended and the dials screwed tight, you had a nice nine-foot long pole. The end of the tool was typically fitted with a curved saw on the end, for sawing branches. Beneath the saw was a lopping shears, for clipping off smaller twigs. Those two gadgets were great for trimming trees…but not ideal for executing killer zombies. So, what's a violence-loving survivor like me to do, once such a dandy tool like a pole pruner has been acquired, but the setup is not quite right for the needed task?

You tweak it, of course. If that someone is like Trick Chasseur, it makes sense to tweak it thus:

Remove the nifty saw. Then remove the neat lopping shears that sat underneath the saw. Toss both items aside. And then you simply install a shaving-sharp machete at the end. A blade that, when brandished correctly, will go through a zombie's neck like a hot knife through…uh, well…yuck…let's just say the machete blade serves well for self-defense.

So, that's a quick once-over to summarize the finely tuned pole pruner I carried. Now, for how I proceeded with that last straggler of the zombie pack which attacked us.

I first removed a heavy leather sheath from the blade, then assembled the killer pole pruner as described; doing this took no time at all. Then yours truly scrambled from the hideout to where the zombie was lurching away in retreat. While my ladies watched from the door of the cellar, I positioned myself in front of the thing.

"End of the line, bud," I said to the zombie. It didn't say anything in reply at first, just stopped dead (is there any other way a zombie stops?) and stared at me. Stared at the blonde-haired human meal it never got to eat. I must say, one look at the young physique I sported, and I think the beast started to become hungry again. Of course, I get that all the time. But I digress. Back to the confrontation…

I didn't brandish the pole pruner. Instead, I let the blade end rest on the ground, holding the center of the pole in a relaxed manner. Saving up a little energy for my attack, but just as importantly, to not telegraph to the opponent what danger lay in the tool I held. Keep the enemy's attention off of the weapon, let the zombie focus rather on my head and neck. Its intended food. Using my own skin, skull, and brains as bait. Not very comforting, but it works.

"OK, bottom feeder. Ol' Trick's got a trick up his sleeve," I said to the mutant.

"Muhh," it said back. Then the zombie trudged my direction, seeming to focus on my head as I'd hoped, its wiggly arms outstretched to seize me.

"Muhh yourself, squishy," I said, then whirled the pole pruner, razor sharp machete leading the way, toward the zombie creature. Aiming above its shoulders.

Slice.

The usual result. After countless real-life executions with the pole pruner and similar armaments, most of my swings are pretty accurate. This particular swipe was no different. One swing with the very heavy gadget, the blade on the end of it designed to chop straight through thick branches, and a detached zombie head thudded to the ground.

I had jumped back from the target as soon as the machete cranked through its neck. As the zombie's body piled up where it had stood, I looked at the air surrounding the action, making sure no blood mist floated my way. None that I could see.

Excellent, so far. One more step remained in finishing off the moaning brain-seeker. The zombie's face was still in action, jaws gaping, making a chomping motion despite being detached from the body.

Could we have left it there, immobile, and just let it dry up and die on its own? Possibly. Some people I've met claim the brain of a zombie must be destroyed, or it lives forever. Don't know for sure, but I think not; rather, seems evident to me that without food or liquid, eventually they'd just die on their own. It's simple logic. They absolutely need sustenance. Why else would zombies so desperately seek food? If you can call the muscle, blood, and brains of living people food.

So we could have moved on and left the undead creature's jaws chomp over and over in desperation, until it dried up or whatever. But that would be unnecessary cruelty. I know these unspeakable, undead beast critters were once people. Human beings who didn't choose the zombie ordeal. So if possible, some mercy is in order when obliterating them. My ladies felt the same way.

Time for the *coup de grâce*. Something I don't savor, but at the same time, I'm good at it. I proceeded.

One fast stab into the temple of the severed head, a

lift-and-smash back to the ground. Another lift-and-smash, then a twist of the blade. The eyes of the zombie head switched from a state of fury to one of unseeing oblivion, and the jaws stopped chomping. Game over.

To remove the machete blade from the thing's skull, I stepped backward and dragged the head along the ground, using the grass and earth as friction, versus using my boot. Why take a chance at contamination? The blade came free, then I thrust the machete point-first into the earth. After working the machete back and forth in the soil for a few seconds, I removed it, then wiped it in the grass to take off any excess dirt. Not the perfect cleansing process, but the best available in a pinch.

Then a final sanitizing touch. I grabbed a small squirt bottle out of my hip pack and sprayed the blade down. The solution – soap, bleach, and water basically – was both valuable and rare nowadays. We'd scavenged the ingredients for the solution over the last year, and were down to this last bottle. Maybe eight ounces left. When it was all gone we'd keep looking for more ingredients, hoping. Best we could do.

After the anti-bacterial misting of the solution, I secured the blade; once intact within its leather sheath, I nodded to each of the gals, who had now joined me outside. They surveyed the just-killed zombie, matter-of-fact looks on both of their faces. Not especially horrified or grossed out. Definitely not that impressed: they'd done plenty similar executions themselves, answering zombie moans with lots of gunpowder and lead.

So…the shooting and killing scene I just described was not that remarkable, especially if one group is unarmed and the other is loaded for bear. You can about imagine the typical chain of events in such an encounter. Did killing zombies – ones which intended to eat us just moments ago – in this way make us some kind of saviors? No. It's not fair when you have a gun and the zombie predators don't. But who cares? Shooting them is the most guaranteed way to put away the decaying threats. The absolute best course of action to take when they attack.

Followed by leaving. And it's best to waste no time doing the leaving, in case more are lured to your location by the commotion. Which they often are. Shoot, kill, then get out of Dodge.

Which we did.

2

The ladies and I had somewhere to be, and we were running late.

We'd been on our way back from an early morning harvest excursion when that last zombie crew struck. The harvest: over the past few years, we'd scouted most of the local region for natural resources that we could scoop up. We know the approximate times during the season certain items ripen, just waiting to be picked and eaten. In this case, some raspberry bushes were due to come into bloom right around then, the end of September. At that time in the North – late summer, almost fall – some of the best berry bursts appear. In these times, such fruit is as good as gold, both for personal food needs and as collateral for trade. We didn't want to miss out. The crop was about a mile from our usual living quarters. A mile's not that far, but even on a short hike you're leaving your fortress nonetheless. Thus leaving safety.

We'd trudged the same route to and from the berry patch. Through desolate neighborhoods, with house after house now gutted, their windows broken, some doors wide open and held there by season after season of sticks, leaves, and crud. Crumbling parking lots crowded with abandoned cars, and items strewn about on what used to be sidewalks. Perhaps they were unwanted things, unneeded and discarded, or maybe possessions lost on the spot when the owner was accosted and killed.

On the way back we came upon an old playground with an ancient, elaborate but now-ignored jungle gym type apparatus. The jungle gym was all covered in vines, the plants embracing and embedding in the metal of the apparatus over the course of what looked like years. I remember seeing a few bones lying just past that jungle gym, including what appeared to be the remnants of a little skull. A human one. The gals didn't seem to notice it. I said nothing, looked away, and continued along with them.

And as it had at one time been suburbia, the area along the route featured the requisite patches of woods, open fields, and a big empty golf course. It was while moving across that forgotten golf course, the grass high enough then to reach my knees, that we were spotted by the gang of ghoulish zombies. Like the berries we'd just picked, Ruby, Margo, and I must have looked tempting for their attack; like big, human, edible, blood-filled berries, just asking to be harvested.

We saw them, just three zombies initially, stumbling from the woods, about 90 or 100 yards away. They had a clear view of us, at least it seemed that way. Regardless, all three of us instinctively ducked and scurried to the tall brush at the edge of the course. Looking to run like hell to escape, or even better, for a place to hide until they plodded past. We spotted the large house and its semi-underground tool cellar, the one described at the start of this tale. The small estate appeared to have been a formerly luxurious house and yard on the edge of the golf course. It was the type that probably doubled as a classic hobby farm, nip and tuck once, but now largely overgrown, being swallowed back up by Mother Nature.

The three of us hustled to the tool shed, found it unlocked, and maneuvered inside. Feeling safe, peering out through a cracked door and a dingy old window, facing out toward the direction of the zombie group, watching them wander aimlessly. Waiting until they left.

Only problem with that approach: they didn't leave.

Later, upon reflection, I realized the wind around the house and shed had been blowing from us to them, and they almost certainly had smelled us. Maybe saw us as well, who knows. As you learned from the preceding events, they certainly stuck around. They did, however, delay their approach, making us believe we were safe for a few minutes. Perhaps they were waiting for reinforcements. You'd have to get inside the head of a zombie to fully understand them and their reasoning. Not recommended.

Soon the horde of hungry undead folks showed up, the first three that we'd come face-to-face with plus a few more, and we'd had to lock up the door and scramble for cover further back in that cellar-like toolshed place I described.

Before that attack, everything was going fine, a lovely September day. Then our trio was caught off-guard. In an unfamiliar place. Plus, within each of our backpacks were large plastic bags filled to capacity with raspberries. We not only had to save ourselves, we had to protect the fruit harvest. The raspberries added bulk to our packs, but even if we'd had the opening to, we couldn't just drop them and run. Those berries, like any other food source, represented life itself.

Yep, the three of us were confronted with some bad luck, so we did what had kept us alive up to that point. We made our own luck. And in the process employed one of my key counterattack policies: we win, they lose.

Yep, we won. After that point, we could finally resume our original plans for the day. To get where we were going in the first place.

Our final lawn cut and cleanup of the season. Summer was winding down, transitioning into beautiful fall weather, typical of the northern parts of the American Midwest. Magnificently sunny yet cool, crisp air. But it wouldn't be perfect weather for long. We'd soon head south, as I've been doing for several years now, Ruby and Margo accompanying me the last two. The three of us would finish up with a certain property's lawn one last time for this season, then go.

You heard that right: we were on our way to report for work. As amazing as it sounds, even in the age of the zombie Apocalypse, the three of us had a job. Specifically, a grass cutting job. And that's where we were now headed.

A job? Why? Well, needless to say, paper money is worthless now. But sustenance is definitely not. Food makes up most of our pay, and it's plenty of incentive. We work and we get to eat, not always a guarantee in this deteriorated world. Will work for food? Damn right we'll work for food. As well as some other things, including medicine, which is in some cases more urgently needed than the foodstuffs.

Our employer? Well, there's only one person left in this entire country – possibly in the entire world – that I know of who can actually provide a job.

And that's if he's not short on his antidote...or if he fails to take it. For some reason, occasionally the urges to transition gnaw away at him, and at times he's tempted to let himself regress into the infected zombie state. Something about giving in to blood lust, he once mumbled. Picturing the act of killing and eating, was what I gathered.

Not good, but anyway. If he takes his meds – which only he knows how to make, by the way – he remains in good condition. Stays in living human form, specifically. And human form for him means a man who's elderly, brilliant, and arrogant; the boss I've come to know so well.

If you've kept up on zombie lore, the chronicles

following the earth's infestation by the brain-hungry mutants, you may already know who I'm talking about.

One Mr. Graves. Mr. Mortimer Graves. Yeah, that one.

Mortimer Graves, the Zombie Billionaire.

3

Mortimer Graves strode forward, peering at us through the openings in his estate's electric fence. He had his shiny maroon cane in hand, as always. Not an accessory he needed, but it rounded out the effect. Complementary to his dark blue suit, which today had a sharp yellow bow tie accompanying it.

Looking sharp for our lunch together…oh, I'm sorry. *Luncheon*. As Mortimer Graves referred to it. We didn't get many of these complimentary feasts from him, served to us no less, but our season was wrapping up and Graves wanted to see us off in style before we headed south for the winter.

Graves came from the side of the mansion where the sun from the south shone most of the day. In line with my guess, he placed a pruning shears on a glass-top coffee table before he reached the gate. Yes, tending to his beloved roses, which bunched up against that side of the mansion, slithering up oxidized copper latticework, glimmering in the sun when in their most peak form. Light orange roses only. No pink ones, no red ones. Just light orange roses. Mortimer Graves was set in his ways.

The roses rounded out his trio of most dearly loved realities: roses, orchids, and swords. Magnificent orange roses, along with delicate, heavenly purple orchids, the former grown outdoors, the latter indoors.

And then there were his swords. Appropriate for a former elite fencer such as Graves, a splendid collection waited inside his mansion. Not just any swords, either. The most prestigious types that he could acquire, longswords and rapiers, scimitars and sabres, purchased back when there was such a thing as international commerce. Wicked steel items from places like Hungary, Mongolia, Belarus, Spain, and Turkey. A couple of precise, delicate blade selections, along with some big, mean-looking bastards. Years back, even before I'd met Ruby and Margo, he'd showed some of them off to me during lunch get-togethers, about a dozen of them or so. I believe he had a few more inside, but entrance to his high-security mansion had become strictly forbidden to other people. Forbidden even for Mr. Trick, your narrator.

Blades, ah yes, lots of them in Graves' collection. One notable item regarding the swords: Mortimer Graves had named them all. Most with the names of one famous historical figure or another. So, yeah, he's into his swords. Enough said on that for now.

The billionaire boy was also something of a chef, preparing savory, elaborate dishes, which if the three of us were lucky, we got to partake in occasionally. Graves had been taught, along with his two siblings, to prepare food and cook it at a high level of skill as a kid. His disciplinarian mother saw to it, assigning each child to be mentored by one or more of the family chefs. She maintained that knowledge of perfect food production and presentation was a necessity to people of their social class. In any case, his mom, dad, and siblings were all long gone now. The chef-level skills were still with Graves, however. He had no love for it, really. He simply didn't know how to whip up meals in any other fashion.

Everybody's crazy about a sharp-dressed man. Make that most everybody, not all. Not me. And in Graves' case, not exactly a man, but rather a sharp-dressed zombie in remission. In any case, appearances matter, always have, and Mortimer Graves was well aware of it. As long as I've known him, he's never been dressed down. No old jeans, flannel shirts, and no cargo pants – that last one amongst my personal favorites. But back to Mortimer Graves, and his suits.

Only Brioni suits adorned his aging body. A type of suit not normally affordable to the unwashed masses, Graves had explained to me once. Elegant, prestigious, tasteful. And in a word, spendy. Not that spendy means much now.

The main character would wear such suits in James Bond films, I guess. Graves had also mentioned that fact. I couldn't care less; I think I saw one James Bond movie total, then the world went to hell in a hand basket. So it's lost on me.

Could fancy suits matter much to me? Ever? Hardly. But to Graves they've always meant a lot. Back in the day, just as the Graves family was about to fall from their pinnacle – not coincidentally at the time the Apocalypse commenced – Graves still had his network. His power structure. His cronies. His need to make an impression. And thus his Brioni suits.

Those cronies in his power structure, in the system, in the elite circles, vanished in short order after the world went toxic with zombies. Some (possibly the luckiest of us) probably were killed outright, others scurried and scraped by, instantly isolated from the top tier that they'd inhabited since birth. Especially since no top tier existed any longer.

And of course, some of those millionaires and billionaires, power brokers extraordinaire, were most likely attacked directly by the dreaded zombies…and were unfortunate enough to survive. To then become infected, and to transition. And to then kill other innocents, maybe eat them.

Oh, man. Becoming infected. For God's sake. Won't ever happen to me, I guarantee it. A handy little 2-shot

Derringer handgun, kept in my backpack at all times, and loaded with a pair of .45 Colt bullets, is my assurance. If zombies kill me and feed on me, not much I can do at that point. But if I'm injured by one, specifically with a bite, and I feel a transition to the dark side coming on, well…the end of the Derringer's going in my mouth. Bam. Goodnight. No zombie transitions in Trick Chasseur's future.

What a world. So many have fallen to the zombie hordes. Either turning into said monsters and doing the eating, or being eaten themselves. My best friends, Toby and Chip, both went down as food to some fucking undead freaks. Neither had the misfortune to become brain chompers themselves, thankfully. This was before the days of Ruby and Margo, the early times, the start of the Apocalypse. Well before I became the killer that I am today. Those innocent times, the ones of my late teens, are gone now though, just like Toby and Chip. Those friends of mine are no more, just like so many others I knew back then. No more, as is hope for most members of humankind.

But there was Mortimer Graves in front of us now, somehow surviving it all. His family's mansion still intact – and even improved post-Apocalypse, now featuring bullet-proof windows throughout. His food production business churning along, allowing him to peddle influence, the principles of capitalism still alive in the Graves lineage. Standing there, simply resplendent in his top-notch suit.

Resplendent. A new word for me; picked it up just recently from one of the many books the gals and I had found and read during our hunts for leftovers. Books are all over the place, and the three of us have read tons of them in our time together. Read 'em and leave 'em. No space in our limited cargo capacity for hauling books around, no matter how excellent. Besides, they get more and more musty every year, just sitting there gathering dust, waiting to be read in abandoned schools, homes, and offices. No other searchers ever seem to grab them. Zombies have no interest in them. Like zombies, the paper books decay with time. But, musty or no, recovered books are a great way to keep abreast of history, plus to use as entertainment as we pass the dead hours in our hideouts. Not to mention, they're great for learning new words, as I've just displayed. Speaking of resplendent...

We waited, watching Mortimer Graves approach. His pallor was about what the vampire of legend was often said to look like: pale, not much living color anywhere on his skin...yet far was he from some kind of dead fish. A strength, a vitality of some kind, lurked just underneath the pasty surface. With a coolness, an unsettling calm, and unshakeable confidence to match. In addition to the suit, a coiffed head of salt and pepper hair was swooshed back over his skull, completing the picture of panache to the end, Apocalypse or no.

Graves opened the heavy gate with his shiny remote control, its sterling silver case giving a glint of the sunlight's energy as he maneuvered it. The Zombie Billionaire stepped out toward us, a pleasant smile on his mostly human face.

4

Mortimer Graves was not alone that afternoon. As far as I know, he never is. Back when workers had been available, he could attract them as employees. Even ones required to live inside the same massive abode as he does, because during the times of the Apocalypse, he had what it takes: shelter, medicine, security. And food. And he could bring in these hires despite being a partial monster man. The wealth and provisions trump the spooky atmosphere of working for a scary boss. He's scary maybe, but Graves has the provisions people need; thus, he often gets his way. What can you say? It's good to be king.

At the time I first met Graves, he'd had a loyal and speedy personal assistant, perhaps a little younger than Graves himself, I'd guess. The assistant guy was probably 65 years old or so. A little over two years after that point, when I returned to Minnesota from my annual winter jaunt to Texas, that assistant was gone, and there was a female servant, maybe age 30 tops. Then another woman helper and a male butler the year after that, both about age 50 I'd guess. Those folks also disappeared in turn, how and where to I don't know. That disappearing thing happens a lot nowadays. Anyway, the first two live-in helpers I'd met had been replaced. That third helper, once gone, created a vacant spot yet to be filled: there just hasn't been anyone around for Graves to hire in such a manner. Few would want to be a maid or butler for an intimidating man like Graves. And of those that may have wanted to, had they had the chance, a large percentage were probably killed off in one way or another before even coming across Graves and his vast resources.

We three certainly wouldn't have considered being his live-in companions or servants. As a matter of fact, at that point I'd never even set foot in his mansion. And in our trio, Graves knew and trusted just me; he kept Margo and Ruby at arms length, formal and polite treatment only. So, no live-ins at the Graves castle were we. We instead lived on his property during the spring and summer, in a big and fairly luxurious pole building. A barn for the hired help. That's right, we stayed in a barn, with a regal mansion hulking over us just 300 feet away.

Hey, who's complaining? The pole building sported high-security windows with heavy-duty steel screens and cast-iron shutters, which could be slammed shut and secured with locks installed into their structure. Plus electricity, which powered lights, a four-coil stove, and several oscillating fans for hot, humid summer weather.

The energy thing was nice. Mortimer Graves possessed an ultra-powerful electricity generator, set up long ago in his mansion's basement. The generator was equipped with some kind of nuclear power block or something; he claimed the electric supply could continue at the current rate of consumption for like 200 years or more. Don't know much more than that, but I did like taking advantage of it.

Another advantage of our living quarters: the barn facility we stayed in for half the year featured running water. Which in this current day is such a luxury the old metal barn seemed like a five-star hotel. Yep, for his lawn-grooming and food-gathering staff, Mortimer Graves aimed to please. Lest we become dissatisfied. And maybe leave and never return. It could've happened any time, and he knew it. He needed people like us.

Mortimer Graves had never offered to let us stay in his mansion, and we were fine with that. Remember, previous members of his staff had vanished. Who knows what had happened to them. I know Graves wouldn't talk about it. So, yeah, the separate pole building we stayed in was fine. Overnight in the mansion with the Zombie Billionaire? I'll pass.

Anyway, the butlers and maids were gone at that point, it seemed for good, but as he stepped out to greet us that day, another mansion resident was at Graves' side. Now the companion at the Graves estate was a dog. And what a dog it was: a goliath named Helmut, mostly Bull Mastiff but with a few other breeds mixed in there – all of them nasty. The big old mutt never seemed to like me, at least not up to that point. As Graves performed his cordial act, greeting us, the huge canine stood by his side, surveying Ruby, Margo, and me as if we'd just stolen his bowl of Alpo. Dogs. More will be said about that grumpy Mastiff beast, the tank with a mouthful of fangs, as my story unfolds.

***

Although never residents on the property of his ominous estate, two more individuals frequented the area near the mansion, performing part-time tasks for Graves. Regular operatives in the region, and not good ones either. I wish I could forget their names, and even forget they ever existed. But they play a crucial role in this tale, and the effects they had partly shape my life situation even now. It would be impossible to tell this story without covering those two morons.

So here are their names: Culp and Clifton. Amos Culp and Kevin Clifton. Schemers, double-crossers, thieves. A couple of bad guys with bad intentions, and unfortunately, they were bad guys with guns. May you ever remember them with distaste in your heart. I know I sure do.

Why did Graves keep them in the employment loop? Why did he help in keeping them fed, giving them the strength to continue with their nefarious deeds? To help them be a source of evil lurking in the background? And lurking practically in Graves' backyard, no less.

It was all about their securing of a product. One he'd assigned them to retrieve, and they'd done so for years on end at that point. They were experts at it. So, you might be wondering, what product? And what about it?

In short, the product that keeps Graves stabilized as a human. The main component in his antidote, the juice that staves off the zombie state. The compound that keeps Mortimer Graves this side of human. Until it wears off. At which point, more is needed.

That main ingredient? A fungus-type growth found on trees. That's all I knew at that point. Lots to learn when your education ends at 17, and zombie hordes descend in place of teachers.

Anyway, the two dipsticks, Culp and Clifton, knew right where the location of the stuff was. Knew just where to find it, how to remove it, and how to package it. Delivering it then to Graves, to allow him to make his mixture with it, and continue to live on. For an extension of life, so he could carry out his nurturing of orchids and roses, his haute cuisine preparations, and not least of all, his attention to that immaculate sword collection. To admire the blades, and to practice with them. All of this was dependent on the fungus-type stuff. Those sons of bitches, Culp and Clifton, had a good thing going.

***

So at that point in time, that pretty much entailed the personalities and operations at the Estate de Graves. Me, Margo, Ruby, the lowlife Clifton, the lowlife Culp, a big hog of a guard dog, and Mr. Mortimer Graves himself.

Oh, and I almost forgot. One more actor played a part in Graves' endeavors. A peculiar little guy who'd been around even before my time. A guy who was instrumental in Graves holding on, in sustaining an existence that at least had a semblance of his former regal lifestyle. That character was none other than one Horace Dunlap, aka the Minnow Man.

Our trio is needed on Graves' estate, for lawn care and for food gathering, but he also has an ally in the form of Horace…er…the Minnow Man, as a procurer of a primary food source. That source is fish, and given the realistic possibilities of what the area offers, those fish are usually in the form of minnows.

The Minnow Man was an expert in a number of things, the main one being the harvest of little, nutritious fish. Minnows mainly, as stated, but also slightly larger scaled prey when possible. If larger fish were present in a body of water and he wanted them, they were in trouble. By hook and line, net, or different kinds of wire fish traps, he'd get them. Word was that the Minnow Man was proficient as well with sewing by hand, for repairs of both nets and clothing. And that he was quite skilled with a fillet knife – trust me, that's an ability to absolutely not be discounted in these times. For food prep. For utility work. And for killing.

It turned out the little guy was an amazing climber, too. Scrambling up trees to retrieve things, but also to escape attackers, I'd heard.

He also has some kind of network of underground tunnels, using these portals to hide and escape from zombies, of course, but also to hide from humans.

Unfortunately, there are plenty of evil souls of the human variety still around. One way or another, the diminutive and mostly unarmed – except for his fillet knife – Minnow Man has this figured out. He's still around, after all.

***

"If you'll excuse me," Graves said, taking a break from his well-mannered small talk.

As we looked in the direction Mortimer Graves was then looking, we saw that the Minnow Man was in fact now with us, appearing from the dense grassy field and its thick bushes without a sound.

"Horace," Graves said to the slender Minnow Man, who then approached us. Graves whispered something to the subdued guy, the Minnow Man listening to each word carefully, ignoring us. Then they both wandered away from us, toward the mansion.

As we sat waiting in the courtyard, the Minnow Man maneuvered through the open gate to the inside of the mansion's grounds. There he hustled, a full-time man of the field, swamps, and underground tunnels. No home other than that. He sported medium length brown hair, a grey long-sleeved tee and faded, formerly black jeans, his clothing beat up but looking fairly clean, considering. His main home may have been underground, but no washed-out mole was he. The Minnow Man's face was tan and a bit sunburned in some spots, due to his spending so much time outside along streams and ponds. Overall the guy looked energetic and healthy. Apparently eating unlimited amounts of fish protein can do a body good.

After the two of them left us so abruptly, Margo wore an expression of curiosity mixed with sarcasm. Not unusual for her. She looked at me with her shoulders shrugged and her expression suggesting the question "Well?" I grinned at her a little, said nothing, and looked over the lawn sections near the mansion that we'd just cut. Admiring it as well as looking for any spots we may have missed. Ruby sat more calmly, but followed the Minnow Man and Graves with her eyes, watching the two to figure out what they were doing exactly. Different reactions from each woman to the two men walking away from us, both ladies wondering what was up.

I didn't wonder. The departure of the two characters was good news to me. I knew what it meant. Graves loved to turn abruptly and leave without explanation. Power play, establishing pecking order, all that. I was used to it. The small talk was secondary now. It was time for them to bring out the food.

And the flowers, as it turned out. The first thing the Minnow Man did, as Graves entered the front door of the mansion, was to walk to the side of the building and approach the lattice work there, its crisscrossed structure covered in roses. The lattice's height went up the mansion's side about 30 feet or so. The Minnow Man scrambled up almost to the top, making it appear effortless. He hooked an elbow through part of the wooden lattice matrix, and soon was hanging by one arm. To me it looked frightful; to the Minnow Man, apparently not.

He slipped the other hand away from the small of his back, a shiny fillet knife now clutched in it. He moved it a few times near a bunch of roses up there, and three of the flowers each with a length of stem attached fluttered down to the concrete courtyard below. The knife disappeared into the back of his jeans again. Must have had a sheath secured down there, and I trust it was a good, solid one. Better have been, judging by the sharpness of the blade. He'd barely touched the rose stems, flicking his wrist a little, and the flowers detached. And who would have known the tiny guy had a serious knife on him at all, much less such a long, sharp slicer and dicer like that?

See what I said about the effectiveness of a fillet knife in primitive times? Would you want to surprise-attack this Minnow Man individual in one of his underground tunnels?

Anyway, the roses arrived on our table. They were contained in a rugged copper vase, its surface partly showing that cool green oxidized look, other parts a dull orange. Those shinier sections on the vesicle glimmered in the sun, matching the radiance of the light orange roses. Enchanting, I had to admit. And knowing Graves, that vase was likely from some ancient, exclusive source. Like some of the collectible trinkets he's shown off from Crete, Majorca, and Cyprus. Wherever those places are.

The Minnow Man didn't leave the premises, not yet. He hustled back to the front of the mansion, and went to a secured door under one of the bay windows that overlooked the courtyard. He undid the combination lock on the front of the door. He entered, then came back out in short order, and walked back to where Ruby, Margo, and I waited. He had a shallow, flat plastic tub in his arms. About the size of a silverware drawer. It had a matching cover on top.

The Minnow Man set the tub in front of us, removing the cover. The tub had three compartments, equal in size to each other. The first held moist, white washcloths; the second had hot, soapy water, soap suds floating on top. I could smell a lemony fragrance from where I sat. I figured the third compartment was warm, plain water, for rinsing. Yep.

We knew the drill, and appreciated it beyond description. A makeshift bath where we sat. For the perspiration, grime, and grass clippings which covered us now, fresh from our two-hour grass cutting job. Clean up for the get-together. Neck, hands, arms. Face. Forehead. Behind the ears. It all felt relieving, not just because of the resulting cleanliness, but also because it helped dissipate the heat our bodies had built up from the lawn work. A thoughtful gesture from Graves, but also a selfish one; he'd told me once in private that he hated to smell human sweat. Those pretentious rich guys. Fussy, fussy.

Welcome also was not just the refreshment from the warm water, but also the rejuvenating smell from the lemon soap. You learn to treasure products like that when you've lived through years of going without. And now the lemon fragrance emanated not just from the bowl of soapy water but also from us, ever so gently. We were just finishing getting clean, as much as we could with clothes on anyway, when the host himself returned.

Graves wheeled a shiny, sturdy cart to the entrance of the gate, then maneuvered it over to where we sat. To where we waited, almost salivating, as smells from the freshly cooked food seeped from the containers. Graves carried out a slick and elegant presentation, per usual. Before he'd left the mansion to approach us with the cart, Graves again used his fancy four-button remote, making an industrial grade metal ramp appear from the curb below the front door. With a quiet whir the ramp extended out a few feet, then touched down to the ground. The catering cart could then roll down it smoothly. Graves steered the cart with a look of ease, and an air of regal satisfaction. From wealthy tycoon to caterer, just like that.

A caterer with good judgment regarding hygiene, I might add. Graves wore transparent plastic gloves reaching up to his elbows, and a surgical mask over his mouth and nose. He always dons these items when playing chef and server. This is in hopes of keeping the food free from any sinister bacteria or viruses...that might actually come from him. In spite of all his outward arrogance and pretentiousness, I think that consideration speaks volumes about the old guy. Despite the bizarre – and dangerous – undertones of a working relationship with such a complex and afflicted man like Graves, it's hard to just turn your back and leave someone like that.

Especially considering the way he can cook.

A scent straight from heaven wafted toward us. The focal point of the cart's cargo was a big stainless steel serving dish. The food was hidden by a heavy rounded cover, the silvery dome clamping down protectively with all its weight over the chow. The steel cover couldn't hide the delicious odors underneath it, though. And I knew the odor well. The three of us did, in fact. It's the nutrient source that kept us healthy and strong all spring and summer in recent years.

Pasta, ah yes. But not just any pasta.

Mr. Graves, the majestic Zombie Billionaire himself, has a process down for making noodles. He whips them up partly from a bundle of ingredients, like cattail roots, green leaves, aspen buds, and wildflowers, but mainly from acorns and maple syrup. He refers to them as "Acorn Maple Noodles." Pretty original name for them, huh? Made from acorns and a maple tree's sweet stuff. How did he ever think of the term? So creative, that Mortimer Graves.

But forget about creativity points for a second, let's switch to nutrition. The noodles, as tasty as they are, don't provide all the nutrients a human body needs. Satisfying for a time, but a whole range of micronutrients is missing if you consume only these noodles. That's where two factors come into play: one, his indoor greenhouse. And two, the agile, scurrying Minnow Man. A commendable array of little plant products are grown in some cellar of the Mortimer Graves mansion, planted and nurtured by old Graves himself. His indoor-grown fruits and vegetables assure any missing plant-based micronutrients.

And the Minnow Man's catches of tiny, medium, and, in rare cases, larger fish supplement things with complete proteins. Once Graves mixes these into a dish, generally the Acorn Maple Noodle recipe, you have serious sustenance. A life-giving, life-saving product. One that nourishes his employees, and one that Graves consequently uses as leverage. The food source allows him to get what he wants. Allows him to secure loyalty.

Yep, Graves was still a businessman; he'd come from a long line of them. It was in his blood. And the most crucial product he deals in was in front of us now: food.

Were we being manipulated? Enslaved? Taken advantage of?

Maybe a little of all those, but really, who cares? Because above all, it was time to feast. We did so many tasks for the tycoon, and risked our lives in the process, for the main benefit of simply being able to eat. Perhaps we were chumps, perhaps we knew it, but in any case, we went along anyway. Based on a principle that always applies, every time.

Yes, this world is not an easy one to live in. Forced to do things you don't want to do. With all the danger, uncertainty, desolation, and hopelessness. With undead cannibals lurking about. Scheming human culprits, too. Even a part-time zombie as our host. All those things to worry about.

But you forget 'em all, when the food appears.

5

Graves ignored us for a moment, and produced a short, round, wide food storage container from the back of the cart. It was the kind people used to use for camping, the type with a dial-on top. It probably held a full quart of food or liquid.

Graves lifted the heavy lid from the serving dish. A veritable mushroom cloud plumed into the air, the steam, the energy, the calories, the scent, all escaping from the feast waiting under the lid. Noodles. Adorned throughout with tiny pine nuts. Sections of bright red chili peppers, subdued green peppers, and cheerful yellow banana peppers – all grown indoors by Graves – had also been mixed into the pasta. Some small fish fillets rested on top, most likely from a mess of runty bluegill sunfish the Minnow Man had captured. The fillets had been glazed in a type of sugary covering, probably Graves' unique clover flower sweet paste. For every fish fillet there were three or four cherry tomatoes resting next to them, the tomatoes also grown by Graves in his mansion's greenhouse. Dandelion leaves ringed the pasta pile, the green morsels soaked for a week in a vinegar solution before serving, their taste rivaling any of the coleslaw made back in the old days. The noodles themselves were swimming in a light-colored sauce, which I would assume was made mostly from liquefied acorns for a butter effect, wild ginger for spice, and maple syrup for sweetness.

And this complete nutritional package was 100% organic, no less.

Graves twisted a fork into one end of the pasta pile,

and proceeded to lift tempting, sauce-covered ropes of noodles upward, which were then lowered into the container. I considered making a run for one of the noodle portions, seizing it from Graves and eating the warm handful of pasta at once. But…Graves was into formality, so there was that pressure making me hold off on the food grab. And I had been doing a great job of giving my ladies the false impression that I knew how to behave in polite company, so the urge to continue that ruse was another factor that restrained me.

Oh, and Helmut, the irritable canine, with his pumpkin-sized head and thousand-pound body or what have you, watched us intently. From outside the fenced perimeter, right by the gate. With no leash. And with plenty of grumpiness. I decided to stay my hand and not lunge at the dog's master. Graves continued to scoop the food into the container.

A minute later, he handed off the sealed device to the Minnow Man, who then retreated to the weeds, out into the Hemlock and Tamarack swamp, where he lives. Now with plenty of freshly prepared grub to fill his gut. Graves turned back to us, and to the serving cart.

He moved in disciplined but smooth swirls of motion, an old skill for the billionaire, serving top quality cuisine that he'd personally generated, an avalanche of it on each plate, each plate from the finest collection available in Japan, he'd once boasted. I ignored the plate's quality, mesmerized as I was by the noodle and veggie matrix it held.

"Have at it," Graves said simply, preparing a plate for himself.

We had at it all right, not looking at each other, not caring what the world was doing for the moment. I barely had time to breathe, so eager was I to swallow the maximum quantity of noodles and assorted goodies.

Go ahead, laugh. If you the reader have something better to eat. And plenty of it. Then go without a full meal for three days straight, or more, as we've done many a time, and get back to me.

After four or five pounds of food, I paused. Breathe in, breathe out. I looked over my shoulder at Margo with her blue eyes, blonde hair tied back in a disciplined bun, then over at Ruby's liquid brown eyes, dark hair fluttering in the early fall breeze. Both of them also catching their breath from the gorging process, a new light of relief on their faces. My women. My partners. My lovers.

And my formidable presence sitting right there to protect them. A good mood in the air already...and once this precious mountain of food was consumed by all, the euphoria would only rise. Who could predict what might happen once night arrived, and we were tucked away in our secure living quarters?

Remember that thing I'd said earlier? About being lucky to be alive?

Time to relax, before the next plate-full anyway. The ready, waiting, hot food had seemed like a dream come true before we'd dug into it. With its fragrance, its heat, its wafting scent. But it wasn't the only scent in the air. Graves had worn his top-shelf cologne for this feast. When you smelled the fragrant elixir wafting from the old boy, you knew he was intent on appearing to be sophisticated. Illustrious. Of discerning taste. Ready for entertaining, hosting, meeting. Negotiating. At times, I wondered if he'd forgotten it was just us he was face to face with. And the Minnow Man, who at times emanated hints of a cologne that could be named something like Eau De Fish Scale.

What was the attention-getting cologne? I'd asked him long ago. He'd simply replied, "Clive Christian." Some kind of cologne company, I assumed. Or maybe some business contact of his family's back when the world was, you know, the world we once knew. Or maybe this Clive Christian was both. Didn't matter. But the old bat was a lot easier to be around when he wore that scent, I know that much.

I decided I had to have some of it. Females liked me without it. But with it...?

"I caught wind of that fragrant stuff again, Mortimer. Your cologne."

"Yes? How's that different from any other time?"

"It just reminded me. I've been wondering. In your chambers or dressing room or whatever you have in there," I said, nodding to his mansion. "Have any extra?"

"You mean, Young Trick, to have a share of some of my irreplaceable cache? For nothing, out of the goodness of my heart. A supply of which, when gone, I'll most likely never come across again?"

"Um, yeah."

"Out of the question," Graves said.

"Possibly as part of a trade deal?" I said.

"Dream on."

Another of my futile attempts to make it into society's upper echelon. The hopes of a rise in prestige: shattered.

"Now, what did you find regarding any strawberries," Graves continued. "Any ready to pick yet?"

"Soon. Most of them are not quite there. Not many ripe ones," I said.

"Scoop some up for me when they are, if you'd be so kind."

We speared more noodles, lanced additional cherry tomatoes with pinpoint precision, skewered another small sunfish fillet periodically. Ah, all the food groups... all you could hope for, post-Apocalypse, anyway. Yum.

"Say, when you're down there in Texas this winter," Graves said. "Could you round up some of those *nogalitos* for me?"

"Oh. You mean those little walnuts?"

"That's right. They are also referred to as the Texas Black Walnut. In any case, bring some back up when you return next spring."

"Well, we generally just eat them then and there. Crack 'em open on the spot," I said.

"Understood. But if you could step it up, above and beyond what you eat, and bring back maybe two dozen. I'd make it quite worth your while," Graves said. I nodded, looked back down at my plate, and retrieved another noodle cluster.

"If you think this sauce is good, wait 'til you try it with five or six of those walnuts mixed in. I ferment the nuts, then puree them. Makes the sauce extra rich."

"I bet," I said, and I meant it. Thinking about all the oils and buttery texture in one of those Texas walnuts, knowing it would only enhance the food quality of a dish like the one we were devouring.

"Learned that method while down there in Texas, actually. A long time ago."

I nodded, said nothing, and skewered a banana pepper with my fork. It didn't last long. *Crunch.*

"Learned the method when I made my first few trips to Texas, with my father and his negotiation team. I think I was 20, maybe 21. All great experiences, but I remember the recipes more than anything. And the gateway to prosperity that opened for us, of course. Without the Texas connection, none of this would have been possible," Graves said, waving a hand at the mansion.

I'd heard it before, but nodded. As did Margo and Ruby. We all knew Graves had almost nobody else to talk to. Merchants who used to pass by to make deals once a year or so had vanished. The Minnow Man was short on conversation. His old live-in helpers were now nowhere to found. That left Helmut, and of course us.

"When I was a fencer at McGill University in Montreal…" Graves said to Margo and Ruby. Blah blah blah. He knew I'd heard the story a few times, and was bored with it. But the ladies hadn't heard it, and since the guy blabbering on was the boss, and host, they listened. It appeared they were interested, but maybe he had them partly hypnotized with his haunting eyes. He could do that; I always looked away after a second or two of eye contact with him. For that reason, when around Graves, I knew I had to keep watch over for my girls. In case things, you know, got out of hand. But other than that, I tried not to look his way anymore than needed.

"You see, the edge of a scimitar, when compared to that of a rapier…" he was saying, while I stared at the roses on his mansion's wall. At the lovely green grass we'd just cut and groomed. And at Helmut, who stared back. As if I was the intruder. And the dog was going to do something about it. Yeah, right, don't get any ideas, dog. I remember thinking that, maintaining the cape buffalo-sized canine's eye contact. I had just got done eating, thus I was not in the mood for Bull Mastiff tenderloin at the time.

I tried to convey this to Helmut with my eyes. *But it can be arranged, ya warthog.*

"It's quite a sword, a real gem…" Graves droned on. "Uh huh," Margo gasped. "Sure," Ruby enthused. I daydreamed.

"With a dangerously sharp edge," Graves continued.

Ah, let me tell you a bit about Graves and sharp edges. Yes, a fencer he had been. In addition, he's expanded his forte, out of necessity. A practitioner with blades back then, and he was still today. As in not only practicing with swords, but also wielding a variety of straight razors. For his precise head of hair, that is. See, hair stylists and barbers are in short supply in the current day. So Graves had to teach himself. Slicing, trimming, adjusting, clipping, until his hair was in its usual stellar shape. He revealed to me that he can cut sections of his hair with either hand. I respect that ability, as in a similar way I myself can wield a knife, club, handgun, or shotgun with either hand. I can punch and Karate chop with either also. Ambidextrous is the way to go.

And as it turned out, he spent hours every month slicing his hair to get it just right. Like it had been in his younger days. For all the social and business activities back then, looking in top form always. With his reportedly lovely and elegant wife, at cocktail parties and ballroom galas, touching base and comparing notes with those of similar high rank. As a business mogul, winning over clients as well as laying down the law, razor cut hair in place regardless. And even now, it was clear that he intended to look his boardroom best until the day he dropped. He wants things just so. Including his precise 'do.'

Mortimer Graves is not necessarily easy to deal with. For one thing, he is always on the edge of transition. Just don't be there when he does change, right? It's not that easy.

At times Graves can seem fine, during the process of normal interactions and social pleasantries. And he can fixate on the person in front of him with what at first seems like a person-to-person focus. The person being the object of his full attention. A stare of appreciation, you could say. But more is going on, I certainly know firsthand, with that stare.

I sense it's nothing sexual. It might in fact reveal urges more intense than even that. Graves never talks of any wishful dreams of meeting another woman, one to replace his long-lost wife. When I inquired one time if he was ever looking for a new wife, he'd replied no, seeming surprised at the thought, more or less. Like there was no interest left in that sort of thing at all. Graves left it at that, and so did I. So I can assume his momentary leering looks betray more of a dietary lust type of thing. Like he's perusing a menu. As in, for things to eat.

"Isn't that right, Young Trick?" Graves said. My thoughts of his eyes and their stare abated momentarily.

"Certainly is," I said with a knowing nod of the head. I had no idea what they were talking about.

Then I heard him mention to the gals about his wish to donate one of his collector swords to my armory. In other words, to give me one. So I would carry it, and use it. Making me, I suppose, one of his knights? Hard to turn down, right? No, at least it wasn't for me. He had weapons that were irreplaceable, hundreds of years old. He wanted to hand one off to me, leaving him with only a dozen or so. But I was more of a pole pruner and machete type of guy. A crowbar or baseball bat guy, the type of person that used his empty shotgun as a club when needed. Or threw rocks. Or kicked enemies in the face. Whatever worked to survive. The collector swords he'd shown me had seemed...well, kind of untouchable I guess. A level of sophistication and quality I had no experience with. How could I slice up enemies with such a precious thing? And what if it got stolen? So, no, I'd turned down his two offers to accept a historic sword to carry. Just couldn't see it.

But, I'll go back to something I'm more comfortable with in this tale. Food.

Mr. Graves himself lives primarily on those Acorn Maple Noodles, the ones I just described. Thank heavens. Ruby, Margo, and I caught fish sometimes, shot a rabbit now and then, and rats even more frequently. The meat from the fish and rabbits went into some of the stir-fries and pastas he'd serve us. The rat flesh went toward dog food.

When we'd hand the harvested creatures over to Mr. Graves, I was always a little hesitant. In past conversations, he'd alluded to the concept of zombie transition triggers. In short, that certain stimuli presented to him started to tip the balance toward transition. I sensed, with some kind of intuition, that this was especially true if there was any blood visible. I'd also bet that hostility and conflict in the air were triggers to some degree. Placid and peaceful was ideal.

In any case, the more vegetarian his diet, the less inclined he is to skip his medication. Fully cooking fish and meat would help to take care of the problem. Undercooking was risky, as consuming such partly raw foods could upset Graves' "balance," let's say. If the balance was tipped too much, all Graves had to do to reach undead bliss, in other words to go fully into a zombie state, was to ignore the injections. To turn his back on the meds, and in so doing, guarantee that he'd go zombie.

Yep, if he passed up the meds too long, he'd transition. Simple as that. And become just one more staggering, moaning, decaying predator wandering around, seeking human flesh. Thus I encourage him to take the medication whenever I see him. And to keep eating those plant sources. Especially his own patented Acorn Maple Noodles. Nice and safe.

Risky things concerning Mortimer Graves and food safety were few. But the risk involving meat was real. I should have recognized a serious danger that day, but I didn't. That particular day the questionable factor was in the form of those tasty fish fillets. Other times such food had been fine with him, but not then. Maybe his zombie biorhythms were off or something.

As we ate the servings of chow that particular day, Graves seemed to be giving his plate's noodle supply short shrift. And his meat source, that day being those sunfish fillets, received his special focus. That was mainly what was going into his mouth. Perilous. I wasn't happy to see it, even then. I should have been more concerned, I now know.

Fillets down the hatch and into Graves' stomach. Four already had been swallowed when he'd started discussing the sword factoids with the ladies, then a fifth one. Then two more from under his noodle pile. He turned the noodles and veggies over, searching for another piece of fish flesh. Ignoring the delightful tomatoes, the peppers, the salad leaves. This wasn't looking good.

He found one last fillet, stabbed it, and popped it into his mouth. He chewed with his mouth open on that last one, a mannerism he never normally surrendered to. Unless zombie transition trouble was on the way. I noted it, but only snickered to myself, wrote it off, and went back to daydreaming. Stupid choice, Trick Chasseur.

6

One of the first signs of a transition with Mortimer Graves was an increased aggressiveness, although at first he could exhibit it within the realm of normal, civilized social dealings. He commenced our get-together thus.

"Anyway, Trick," Graves said. "And ladies. There was mention of a trade deal just moments ago. An impossible one, regarding my irreplaceable cologne."

We waited. Graves had assumed a different posture now. No longer the conversationalist, the chef, the server. Instead, he'd now taken on his favorite pose: Chairman of the Board. It meant something was coming. A proposal, or instructions, or a decree. "There's another trade deal, a realistic one, I'd like to mention. Which is fitting, since you three will be in on it," Graves said.

I said nothing. We waited some more. This could be good. Or, not so good.

"You recall the characters Amos Culp and Kevin Clifton?"

Not so good.

"You're familiar with them?" Graves asked.

I knew them. And hated them.

"Yep," I said.

"Our local roamers, jacks of all trades you could say," Graves said.

Yeah, you could say that. You could also say thieves, con artists. Muggers of helpless travelers.

"They'll be partnering with you on this."

"Says who?"

"Says them. Says me. That's what we decided upon," Graves said. "To increase efficiencies."

I was taken aback. Graves partnering with those two dweebs? Possibly affecting his relationship with me?

"They've brought in a certain product for me over the years, and have always done a proficient job," Graves said. "Time is short with the three of you about to head south. Harvest of some items, mainly acorns, is behind schedule."

It wasn't. I wondered why he wanted to step up the hoarding of the nuts, crucial as they were, to an unrealistic level. I never really found out. Greed? Maybe. Perhaps he just couldn't let go of the old ways, from back when his family had an actual empire. Not just Graves all by himself, on a lovely patio in the sun, sharing portions of his pasta recipe with employees. Pretending he was still some kind of overlord.

"So you, what, you sat them down to break bread like now, and decided all this?" I asked.

"I never feed them. I give them their supplies as payment, then I want them to get lost."

An uncomfortable silence ensued. Just the clinking of forks to plates, the three of us twirling a second helping of noodles with efficiency. Chomping on the pasta clumps, spearing cherry tomatoes and chili peppers, with the sweet acorn sauce making overeating irresistible. Stuffing our faces. A necessary habit: you never knew when the next chance at plenty of food – or any at all – would present itself. I waited until my last bite was fully inhaled before speaking.

"I don't like it," I then said, with full bravado. But with nothing to back it up. I didn't make the rules at the Graves estate. Not that I always remembered that.

Mortimer Graves zeroed in on me with perceptive eyes; knowing ones, experienced ones. Eyes that had been traveling the world, closing deals, putting out fires for his family's empire. When I was a just punk, as a boy, then a teen, trying to catch fish, shoot a deer, kick ass in Shotokan Karate, and later maybe get laid for the first time. All while he saw the world – from places like Moscow, Tokyo, Shanghai, Geneva – start to change... break down...collapse. Even before the Apocalypse ever hit.

"Well Trick, my friend, that's the way it's going to go down. Harvest time is coming to a close. The three of you will not be enough," Graves said.

"And if not?" I said. "If we decide to do it alone? Without Culp and Clifton?" At that particular moment, I was not nearly old enough or experienced enough to realize that ultimatums were a losing proposition. That ultimatums were preposterous. If you had the guts, or the ability – or the ammunition – to do something, you just fucking did it. No ultimatums. No showing the other side your hand.

"Well then, Mr. Chasseur, there's the highway," Graves said. He nodded to the area just past the expanse of field in front of his mansion. Two hundred yards away lay the concrete ribbon, the one I remember from my childhood, the highway that had always led from the northern suburbs down to Minneapolis. Now just an expanse of concrete littered with trash and the remnants of vehicles. And with bodies, some so old now that they were nothing but dehydrated, flat piles. Tiny grey speed bumps. I'd flown over and around them many times on my cycle, and not once had I let myself think about what those scatterings of matter really were. It was just residue. Just detritus. I kept looking that direction. Not knowing what to do or say next. Not wanting Ruby or Margo to see any doubt in my eyes.

"The three of you did such a tremendous job last spring securing all that maple syrup. It paid off for me, and certainly paid off for all of you. Why not keep a good thing going? You know how these things go," Graves said. "You've negotiated plenty with me yourself, Trick."

"But Culp and Clifton? They're creeps. Crooks. Thugs. I'm not a thug."

Graves lowered his fork, settling his gaze upon me. Which was, well, unsettling. Perfect liquid blue orbs, set against strongly sculpted face bones. Centuries of selective breeding may have made a handsome face, but it couldn't hide in those eyes something a little…not of this world.

"Oh?" was his only comment, the eye contact remaining. Then he switched his glance over to Ruby, then to Margo. Enjoying the vision of them was my guess. I started wishing, quite forcefully, that he would quit it.

Hey, Graves: they belong to me.

"Well," I replied, "maybe sometimes. But only as needed." Knowing he may have had a point with the thug comment. Knowing that I may have been a little heavy-handed a time or two.

He looked back in my direction. Then, once again, the closest thing Graves could muster to a smile appeared on his lips. His eyes, however, did not smile, maintaining instead a superior, knowing look, and still sending out signals that were…again, almost hypnotizing, you could say. Like one of those magic snakes of legend soothing you with its stare. Before it constricts you.

Time to wrap up lunch.

7

We soon retreated to our seasonal lodging, and got ready to settle in for the night. The modern day barn, in other words a big metal pole building, was simplistic, but during the summer season, the place was home. As long as Mortimer Graves allowed it. He sure supplied it. As mentioned earlier, the barn featured electricity. Along with three twin beds. Pillows. Blankets. A simple bathtub, and a nice oversized sink. A small station, plus ingredients, for making organic soap. And oh, that running water. Hot water if we wanted it, too. Amazing.

We were outfitted with protection there too, above and beyond our guns and my machete-on-a-stick. As I stood there that evening, looking out into the darkness and thinking, I leaned against the window's metal grate, a kind of metal webbing of sorts that covers all of the windows in our living quarters. I made sure the electrical charge to it was deactivated before touching it. See, Mr. Graves, the planner that he is, knew that things…read zombies…would try to get through the windows of our pole building eventually. So the grates that covered each window of the building were highly electrified. We could control it from the inside with a lever. On or off. All or none. I don't know how many amps or volts or whatever the dense screens could carry. But do you remember those bug zappers from the old days? Where the hanging, fluorescent bulbs would lure bugs in, then sizzle them upon contact. Well, that's what happened to zombies if they touched the screen when the charge was on. Kind of cool and horrifying at the same time. A few left the area with smoking hand stumps, or maybe a smoldering nose now and then.

Howdy, zombie friends. You can look but you can't touch. Ha.

The big barn was perfect for storage as well. It was where we kept our motorcycles, among other things. We get out on foot and trudge most of the time, as it's just more workable and flexible. Plus, there's no set of wheels to take care of if you walk. But we needed vehicles for longer trips, providing there were passable roads where we were going. Those usable roads are getting fewer and fewer with every year. But you use what's available.

We kept the bikes stored inside. Zombies couldn't care less if they were left outside, and won't touch them, except for a rudimentary inspection due to the slight human scent the bikes might hold. So, few worries there. But there are plenty of people still left on earth. Not all of them are good either, as you'll soon see. They'll steal all sorts of things, a cycle included. Or just certain parts from one. That can be almost as bad.

You need all of a machine's working components to be in order, more so now than ever. There are no longer roadside mechanics to assist a person. You may need to scavenge the parts from orphaned cycles, if you can find the right models sitting somewhere. Solid, working tires are also necessary, and thankfully easier to find than the smaller parts, crossing over brands as tires sometimes do. Another requirement to keep rolling: clean, usable oil for the motorcycle's engine. And of course, you need fuel.

For those last two components, we definitely selected a good person to have as boss.

Graves has the knowledge, ingredients, and machinery to make a gasoline substitute. A primary ingredient used to make the fuel is spent motor oil. How convenient, right? And, it's not only convenient, it's not really that much of a coincidence.

You see, the Graves family's dynasty was built on oil wealth. Their clan started the real snowballing of wealth and influence with small steps. Buying holdings in the Bakken formation, a cluster of massive, ultra-valuable oil fields mainly in North Dakota. But that part about acquiring shares and rights was just normal investing for the already wealthy Graves clan. Things soon improved for them exponentially, with some risk taking, some insight, and some arm-twisting. I can relate to that last part in my own endeavors. Wink. But I digress.

It turned out that areas in both Manitoba and Ontario, provinces just above North Dakota, had similar formations. Ultra-precious, and completely unknown. Not known about for the first seven or eight million years of their formation, that is. The Graves family spies – oops, I mean researchers – uncovered these facts with a few payoffs and some pressure to key scientists who were looking into the geology there. Just on the little information they could glean, the decision was made to go Ultra Bakken, you could say. With an existing Texas business partner, they arranged distribution in the south, then throughout the Gulf. Once that was squared away, they then bought the land in Manitoba and Ontario that contained the oil reserves. It was dirt-cheap at the time. They acquired it before a single competitor could bring up the fact sheet. Before a single hole was drilled for the newly discovered oil. Before anyone realized the oil was even there.

Except, of course, for some traitor scientists. Some of who didn't want certain secrets of their personal lives revealed. Better the irreplaceable oil reserves were uncovered than their unseemly behaviors. And for all of the scientists involved, their principles and oaths apparently didn't overcome the vision of lots of easy greenbacks. Already laundered, of course. For those scientist weenies: secrets remained secret, and their checking accounts swelled with gifted money.

For the Graves family: oil dynasty. Prestige. Wealth beyond compare in their social circles. Influence that went unquestioned.

All remaining in place until, of course, the zombies hit. Oh well. Insert Trick Chasseur chuckle here.

That's the background of Graves and his wealth in abbreviated form. But back to Graves' present-day operational details, specifically the fuel that he supplies us with.

The main source to make the gas is already-used oil, which he has massive vats of underground. Once made, the stuff smells and looks like normal gasoline…a smell everyone born after the age of William Shakespeare knows. But it's actually not the standard gasoline of old. Since he mixes the gasoline-like bromide with a bit of explosive nitroglycerine, just a teensy bit, it allows the fuel in a liter – not a full gallon, just a liter – to go a long way. And really makes our cycles fly. Hot damn. Only small amounts of the stuff are needed. A complete gallon would last almost forever in a motorcycle.

The fuel that Mortimer Graves can provide to motivated laborers – such as my ladies and me – is of the utmost importance; it's actually the second most significant product he bargains with. Food is first, naturally.

You have to have fuel to ride, to propel the motorcycle under you. And food to stay alive in the first place. Fueling bodies and bikes: our employer knows how to fill those needs. It anchors us for the season. It keeps us coming back.

And those motorcycles are ideal. We could have some monster SUV or extended cab pickup, for sure. They've been abandoned all over the countryside. Some with both keys and skeletons inside. So yeah, we could have one, and we'd drive it less than a couple of days before the fuel was expired. Not good.

So it's the motorcycles. I turned from the window and took a look at my beauty of a roaring beast in the far corner of the barn. A rip-snorting Kawasaki Vulcan, just eager to be opened up on the lonely highway again soon. Wine-colored, huge, shiny, with a spacious double seat. So Ruby could sit on back and clutch me, keeping me warm while I excited her with my masculine vibes. And you'd maybe assume that Margo alternated into the passenger scheme here, taking turns with Ruby for a chance to hang onto Mr. Dynamic as we'd ride. That does occur with our lovemaking rotation, but not with riding. No, Margo had her own. She'd have it no other way.

Another Kawasaki? Or some other sensible Japanese work of precision, easy to fix, rarely breaking down, parts all over the place if needed? No. She could have selected one of a hundred different cycle designs, but Margo of course had to have one displaying prestige. A BMW. Surprise. They used to refer to BMW cars as Broke My Wallet brand. The cycles appear to be no different. There aren't any wallets to break in the present day, but I've nearly broken a knuckle or two fixing that sonofabitch of a bike over and over. When it runs, her motorcycle really hauls ass, every bit as fast as my Vulcan. But still.

In any case, BMW, Kawasaki, or just about any other brand definitely beats what used to be number one in American cycles. You know, that former stalwart of supposed tough guys. The one, the only, the Harley Davidson. Some used to assign them the nickname Hardly Able-son. I would agree, with experience to back up the opinion. I tried one of those for a few tiresome months. I guess some folks used to see a Harley and feel the call of the open road. I think about one, and I feel the call of an open toolbox. I also remember some of the lame t-shirts Harley fans would wear. Like "Mess with the best, die like the rest. Harley Davidson." Sure. I think they were referring to the Harley cycles themselves. Dying.

Leader of the pack? A lot of the chunky guys I used to see years ago riding Harleys looked more like Lead Me to a Big Mac.

Anyway, I've got a lightning fast Vulcan. If it breaks down irretrievably, I'll find another one. Or something similar. Or put a bunch of parts from several cycles together and design my own. One piece at a time, and it wouldn't cost me a dime.

But, enough about cycles. Currently my mind was on our armaments. Our guns. And our dwindling supply of the necessary diet for those weapons.

At that point, things were going pretty well, although there was a nagging problem I had to solve. Or not. We were low on ammunition. Graves has lots of resources, but ammo isn't one of them. I'd always wished he had a method for gunpowder production, but he hasn't the first clue. I guess too much time of his has been spent on devising the best way to make gourmet dishes, dreaming up tactics with the somewhat limited ingredients that could be brought to him. And on his sword collection. And pampering his big, hungry dog like it's the child he never had. And his orchids. And roses.

I have the main ingredients for the manufacture of gunpowder, except for one: it's a substance called elemental sulfur. The other stuff I know I can find in the north, from naturally occurring sources. Inexhaustible quantities of it, actually. But the elemental sulfur was available only in certain places. And not in the north.

Thus the "or not." You can't wave a wand and make resources appear.

But that stuff, the elemental sulfur, was to be had over a pretty wide range throughout Texas. There are beds of it in certain places in the ground, and we overturn rocks there in the hopes that their undersides contain the residue. We also examine little pebbles nearby, and score with those as well. Over the course of a few days, we could scrape off a half-pound of it or so into a plastic bag, and realize a nice supply for making ammo for the next few months, if not more. Not that difficult. But you have to already have ammo to protect yourself as you collect the stuff, and also while you're filling new cartridges. And...you have to be where the ingredients occur. In our case, Texas over the winter.

See, we don't leave Minnesota in October every year just because cold is coming. It's also to be down where the missing gunpowder ingredient is. We need it, we get it, then use a primitive pestle and mortar to grind each ingredient into a fine powder. Reload new ammo using spent cases. Put either lead BBs or buckshot into the shells for projectiles. Or if those aren't available, taconite pellets we find on old railroad tracks can be used. Once done, when we're back to being locked and loaded, we can feel the power of the gun coursing through our veins again. Then enjoy pleasant winter weather, and engage in trade with a number of pretty cool Texans that I know. It's all good...except every fall when I go down there, at least one of the folks I used to interact with is gone. No one else seems to know where to or why.

Plus, there's always plenty of shooting we have to carry out. Texas was a massively populated place at one time (with people), so it allowed that many more folks to become infected and go zombie. Zombies with a southwestern twang, if you can imagine. It's tragic...but good target practice. What can you say? Anyway, when the hellish Texas summer heat is just around the corner, we motor back up to the bursting green of the northern spring. We're Apocalyptic snowbirds, more or less.

Basically I love my shotgun, and need it, but hate the problem of ammo shortages. I came up originally in the world of weapons – other than my fists, feet, and head-butting skull – with a weapon that needed no gunpowder. No bullets. I still have a couple of models of that very weapon, right over in a storage locker on the east wall of our barn. I'm an expert with said weapons. But now I never use them.

Bows. So beautiful. So primal. My choice had always been the recurve bow. You know, the wooden kind shaped in a curvy wave formation, like the old books show Robin Hood using. Not the compound bow with pulleys and cables and an auxiliary joist for the release mechanism or whatever the hell they use. Just a wonderful, layered length of gorgeous wood, bent over into a tight curve, with a string looping around each end. Ready to shoot. Ready to kill. But to kill…with arrows. Like our bullets and shotgun shells, the bow's "ammo," in other words the arrows, posed a problem.

For a few years, my backup at all times, especially in the case of an ammo shortage, had been the described recurve bow. For arrows, I used aluminum rods, taken years ago from an abandoned home improvement store that sold window coverings. For the broadheads on the end of the arrows – broadheads are the cutting tips – I devised a system for using triangular pieces from some wrought iron lawn furniture. I just used a hacksaw to get some small, strong, easily-sharpened wedges from the iron tables and chairs, then attached them to the end of the window treatment rods with a homemade glue, mostly made from pine sap.

But that was then. We just couldn't keep up with the need for new arrows and their tips. Heck, powder-filled shotgun shells were easier to acquire. I hated to turn my back on archery, but it just evolved that way.

The pole pruner, tipped with the accessory of a zombie-beheading machete, had nowhere near the range of a bow. But up close, the machete was so much more convincing. It especially got their attention once their zombie heads would hit the ground. It was a decent substitute for arrows. And the shotguns and less commonly used rifles blew the archery stuff away.

So the bows were put away, now collecting dust. My lovely, beloved bows. Years of practicing with them, inching up my skills. Proven in real life with many hefty feasts enjoyed after killing deer with the arrows the bows flung. Compared to a super-alert deer, killing a zombie with a bow was a joke. Almost too easy. But no more. Until people of the post-Apocalypse somewhere set up an arrow-making business, the bows will stay inactive. There's simply not the time nor the materials to go on with archery as a self-defense option. One more disappointment for me in the present world.

Why did this zombie shit have to befall us?

***

Of course, we had to count our blessings. In addition to the noodles and the fuel, Mr. Graves has a method to make antibiotics, a formulation quite similar to penicillin. Another possible life-saver, in some cases. He simply refers to it as "penicillin-plus."

Graves figured out the medicine angle, probably out of necessity. Then people like my partners and I came along, and a business ace like Graves knew his antibiotic potions would be in great demand in our minds.

Capitalism lives on at times, even in this zombie-filled world.

Intrepid adventurers like our trio get cut, scraped, and nicked all the time. In the zombie land world, getting a severe infection could be almost as bad as getting rabies or whatever you want to call it from a zombie mutant. The death may be fast, or may be slow, but as a bad infection spreads, the pain might be so bad you just kill yourself to end it all. So I've been told. Penicillin-plus can stave off an infection and save the day.

How does Mortimer Graves make the penicillin solution? Well, hard to know exactly, but you don't make premium fuels from oil, as his family did for 60 years, without some precision application of chemistry, biology, physics, and some very exacting lab procedures.

Those factors all play a part in making the medicine. But just as importantly, all of them focus on one key ingredient, one that is absolutely critical to the making of the penicillin-plus. Critical to production of his valuable drugs, and critical – absolutely so – to how this very story you're reading unfolds.

There are three key points to make about this special ingredient. One, I didn't yet know exactly what it was. We were out of the loop on that ingredient's name or origins, thus powerless in its supply and demand. Graves could keep its value high in that way, and require plenty of either labor or harvested products from us for the exchange of penicillin-plus.

Two: it was also a necessary ingredient for the antidote Graves used to stop any transitioning. Its need by Graves was therefore crucial, if he wanted to stay in human form.

Three: the main, maybe only, suppliers of the ingredient to Graves were the two forms of human refuse known as Culp and Clifton. They had the ability, knowledge, or perhaps the secret to this ingredient. Where to get it, how to procure it. What it was in the first place. Thus the value of these two men to Mortimer Graves.

How Graves makes the antidote I also have no idea. I've never needed the potion injected into me, thankfully, but I do have access to it in one respect. A strong dose of it that Graves supplied to me himself. Just in case. And not for me. For him.

Per Graves insistence: I keep a hypodermic needle filled to the top with the antidote, set inside a small reinforced case that clamps shut. All safe, secure, and unbreakable. That case containing the heavy dose of antidote goes into my hip pack, and never leaves it when I'm up north, in the territory of the Zombie Billionaire. In case that zombie portion of his nickname comes to life.

***

I looked back out the protected window over to the Graves mansion, seeing just one light on in there. Looked lonely. Just Mortimer Graves and the big dog with an attitude. The Minnow Man resided in the direction opposite, out deep in the dark swamp somewhere. In a tunnel or cave, protected. Alone, as he seemed to prefer it. I didn't know how they were doing, but I personally was feeling wonderful.

Ruby and I had made love a little earlier in the night. Margo had rested or went to sleep or whatever. Next time it would be Ruby resting, sitting out, however you want to refer to it. Do I sit out? No. And none of that two women at a time stuff. I've never done that, and wouldn't even have known where to start with a couple of them at once. Not sure why I would, with half the reason for engaging in sex being to reproduce. I have the drive of lust, all three of us did, but there's some kind of higher calling going on. I feel it, and both women said they felt the same. Somebody somewhere has to get the repopulation started. Might as well be us three, we'd thought. Hadn't happened yet, but we held out hope.

How do you proceed with a pregnancy and baby in this world? Not sure. We'd figure something out, we knew.

I kept busy when copulation was possible. Two of them, and just one Trick. Works for me.

Does that make me a cad? An opportunist? A chauvinist? If you have the luxury to think like that, you're not living in the same post-Apocalypse as us. We've went days without so much as a bite of food. At times, especially on the road, we've been without water, or at least not water that we thought our portable water filters could make safe. And I went hungry and thirsty all the time, year round, before I made the connection with Graves, his mansion, and the related jobs he offers. And even when water and food are available, we get chased. We shoot, club, and sprint our way out of deadly trouble. Life in the post-Apocalypse ain't easy. So we get it on when we can. Seize the opportunity when there's down time and plenty of food and drink. That's not as often as it might seem.

And frankly, all three of us were lucky we had a companion of any kind, someone we could team up with and trust, much less make love with. And we knew it. We proceeded accordingly. I believe I didn't bring it up as much as I should have to them, but I lived with the knowledge that I'd be long since dead if not for my two women. I don't mean "dead" figuratively either. Saving me for real, with alertness, assertiveness, and firearms. Three times specifically: saving me from one human and two zombies, total. Ruby once, Margo twice. Even a blond, virile superman of the post-Apocalypse can falter and be caught off guard. Which kind of means I'm not really a superman. But I like to practice positive self-talk.

Ah, women. My main requirements in a woman? In today's partly undead world, if she breathes, it's a good start. And there I was, in that moment not only with two of them, but each woman a dream girl. For me at least. Well, back then Margo was often equal parts dream and nightmare. But things worked out over time.

Example: an incident that very night. Earlier, there'd been a little discomfort in our happy little trio. A conflict. Ruby didn't get involved, as often was the case, remaining more the onlooker. A tussle of sorts just between Margo and me. Margo's fault, as usual. Not mine. By design, I'm generally blameless.

It started just as we were settling in, our stomachs now chock full of nutrients from Graves' generosity. Feeling at ease, satisfied.

"Who are these supposed bad guys?" Margo said. "This Clifton and Culp duo…I gather these guys have a reputation as being suspect."

"That's something I have to talk about to the both of you," I said. "We'll cover it soon."

"What have they done? Are they thieves or what?"

I didn't answer Margo, and instead remained quiet, focusing on my strategy for proceeding. If these guys, Clifton and Culp, were really bad news, why was I allowing the ladies to be put at risk? Were they actually bad news? Yes. Very. Like shooting people in the back after they'd earned their trust type of bad news. Graves had insisted though. The half-zombie bastard. I was caught in the middle. Not something I liked. Not something I often allowed.

"We're waiting," Margo said.

We're waiting.

I stopped concerning myself with the answer, and with how to phrase it exactly. I fixed Margo with a steady stare, until she looked down and away. As expected. That occurrence of micro-intimidation from me wasn't unusual. I had to keep control of situations, manage other people, men and women both. I still do. It's all about keeping things running smoothly, not about being a bastard or whatever. Who's got time for arguments and attitude…when at any time we could be eaten?

I still hadn't said anything, thinking it over. Then her pride, her arrogance, won over. She looked up, and back in my direction.

"Cat got your tongue?" Margo said.

That was it. People didn't intimidate this guy, and they sure the fuck didn't say things to me like *we're waiting* and *cat got your tongue?* Not even Mortimer Graves. At least not without risking my abandonment of them.

"Like Graves said, my sweet, the highway's right over there," I said.

Silence. Again. For an instant I hoped a zombie would attack the building or something. Provide a distraction. None did. My saying it that way was too harsh, way too severe, to utter to an ultimate insider. One of my women. They don't grow on trees.

Margo didn't say anything in return. She didn't scream. Or swear. She just turned over, and went sullen. Motionless on her little twin bed. Looking deflated.

Did she have to be so pushy? Ask such prying questions, to which I didn't have easy answers? Actually, she did. She had every right. Margo probably assumed, correctly, that these dweebs were serious trouble. Especially once seeing the tension between Graves and me as we discussed the other men. And what were the odds that they wouldn't be trouble? It was the post-

Apocalyptic way, after all.

So I soon found myself a little while later, all alone by the window. Staring out to the pitch-black fields, to the light that burned in the mansion. Thinking. And I turned to click off the final bedside lamp, which lit up our living quarters, to make my way to my own single bed, the small but welcoming mattress. For rest. Sleep. Oblivion.

And there was Margo, wide awake, meeting my eyes, staring at me from her own mattress.

"You owe me an apology, moron," she said. Quietly though, as to not wake the sleeping Ruby. The low volume of her silken whisper added an atmosphere of civility, I must admit. I couldn't summon any anger whatsoever in response to her insult. Especially since she showed consideration to our other companion as she did it. And really, an insult wasn't so bad when you knew what might await you outside in the dark. Pretty tame, that insult was, compared to the fangs of a zombie. I sometimes forgot that, but just then I grasped the big picture, retained the proper perspective.

"Elaborate," I said.

She wouldn't. Margo just lied on the bed, obstinate. Just staring at me. Not responding. Then she flipped over, away from me. Again. Using her precious energy to ignore me. Who was to rectify this situation? It always fell to one person.

Leader of the pack. So strange that I'd thought of that very phrase just moments earlier. Of course, in our tiny group that leader was me. Before, with other people, including other young men I teamed up with, it had also been me. None of them wanted to step up, whereas I wouldn't want it any other way. So cool to be in charge, right? In certain instances. But sometimes it sucked.

Margo was having a temper tantrum in the world of

the zombie. Amazing, isn't it? We couldn't afford it. Not the conflict, not the wasted efforts, the unneeded hostility. I'd have to fix it. Time to play Mr. Interpersonal Communication. The peacekeeper. Trick Chasseur, he of the double barrel shotgun, high-impact karate kicks, and the flailing machete. Me, of all people!

Ugh. Here we go.

8

"I should have known better than to get involved with a blonde airhead," I said. Not a great opening line, I admit. But you have to set the tone.

"You think you're some kind of rocket scientist, Trick?" Margo said. "On top of it, you're blond too."

"Yeah, but I'm...me." I kept it rolling, showing who was who.

"So superior, aren't you? What entailed your life, before all this Apocalypse crap hit? Beating people up in Kung Fu—"

"Shotokan Karate," I said.

"Yeah, OK. Taekwondo Karate or whatever you just said. And shooting guns and bows. Shooting at deer..."

"I hit some."

"And getting satisfaction from it I bet," Margo said.

"Yeah. Plus I got full from eating them," I said.

She gave pause; she couldn't contradict that part. All three of us ate any deer...or rabbit, or pheasant, we could intercept nowadays. Plenty of them were left, but we had plenty of things getting in our way of pursuing them. Margo gave her pause for a few seconds, then carried on with her fusillade of disapproval.

"So you focused on sports, hunting, shooting, charming the girls, and violence."

"Violence should come earlier in the list."

"Yeah, I know. So that makes you a profound individual?"

I shrugged and smiled.

"So I'm the airhead. You're the master. Yet you had a life based on punches, kicks, gym culture, bullets, and babes."

"I was young."

"You still are, and you're still a prick. You order us around, as if…"

"You know you like it," I said. I smiled with one side of my mouth, the smirk thing. As planned, it threw Margo off. The smile flickered in her blue eyes, the same almost occurred on her mouth, but she clamped it shut tight. Fighting it. You go, girl.

"Flip over, Suzy Sunshine," I said.

"Why? What you got up your sleeve now, tough guy?" she said, performing the scolding, disapproving act. But she still flipped on over to her front, didn't she?

I rolled up one side of the blousy cotton sleepwear bottoms she wore, to the point that her whole lower right leg was bare. The pants, I think they had been nurse scrubs originally, had been discovered by the ladies at an abandoned hospital last year. Nice find. Two pairs each had been collected, I think.

"Where's it sore?" I said, beginning to knead her calf muscles, otherwise known as the gastrocnemius, and the muscle triangle under it, the soleus muscle. On the road I'd come across some bodybuilding books. I told you I read when I had the chance.

"How'd you know it was sore?"

"You were bitching about it during the lawn work," I said.

"I mentioned it to Ruby. I didn't even know it registered with you."

"You don't think I hear things?" I replied. She said something else, it didn't sink into my tired brain, and I ignored it. It was time to get to work. My hands and forearms had been trained for years almost nonstop with heavy dumbbells, high-tension archery equipment, and martial arts techniques. Most of that had since went by the wayside, now replaced with steering lawn mowers and motorcycles, as well as wielding a shotgun and a deadly pole pruner. I still had it. My dexterity was intact and my clutching ability strong. Margo would now benefit. The massage began.

Sure enough, two knots revealed themselves on the outside section of her calf. I worked them out in short order. Squish, steady pressure, glide, squish, steady pressure. I kept it up until those swellings leveled out, then navigated to the rest of that lower leg. In the center, up to just below the knee, then to the inside section. Let my hands squish and glide on down, to the area below the main calf muscles, then all the way to the ankle region. I could sense the effects on Margo, not only on her leg, but on her entire being. Relaxation, then a slight recoiling in pain when I did the pressure thing, then more relaxation and a kind of vanquished joy when a given area was done being pummeled.

This pleasure-pain was not new to Margo. Nor to Ruby. My massage tactics are all self-learned, but I think I've figured out a good system. It's to impart relief and bliss, yes, but it's also a way to keep beat up bodies in viable condition. I never voiced it to them, but I saw this as not just a nice thing to do, but also as part of my duty. Taking care of my women. My loved ones. And let's face it: I wasn't a saint by doing these rubdowns. I was essentially returning their dedication to me, their love and care, which I sometimes took for granted.

"So I should still hit the highway? That what you think?" Margo said finally, in a subdued mumble.

"Is that what you want?" I said.

"Of course not."

"Then it won't happen. Not on my watch," I said.

Margo stayed quiet, the only response being seemingly greater relaxation in her body after I said it. I remained quiet too, for another minute, the massage squishes and pressures delivered by my hands continuing.

"If you're hitting the highway, it'll be with me," I continued. Probably more of the olive branch Margo was looking for. Seemed to sit better with her than calling her an airhead. I sometimes got it right. Well, I was learning on the job, what can I say?

Eight more minutes on the sore leg. I lowered that leg to the bed in slow motion, then scooped up the other leg. Slow motion still. That leg of hers didn't hurt apparently, but nothing wrong with preventive maintenance. Up with the pants leg, revealing smooth, warm, female skin. I bet you're starting to believe me less and less about what a tough job I had.

Glide, squish, steady pressure. Over and over. She remained motionless, until her body twitched with the first throes of sleep. Breathing becoming heavier. Down with the fabric of the pants leg. I lowered her limb back to the mattress, and rose from the bed without a sound.

I stepped over to the lever on the wall and turned the juice back on for the metal window grates. Then I clicked off the last lamp and stumbled to my own little bed, where I collapsed into oblivion.

9

So there we were. Ruby, Margo, and I followed Graves' directive, and took a chance, just once, on a cooperative venture with Culp and Clifton; just once, and as I had guessed in advance, it was regrettable.

The previous year, Mortimer Graves had issued a definite – but unclear – warning about them. Mr. Graves told me in a brief discussion that Amos Culp had been a cop. And that Kevin Clifton had served as a soldier, an Army grunt of some kind I believe.

Details about the two guys had been sparse in Graves' rundown on the details. But he hinted at a few things. "They have their own set of rules," Graves had said. "Be careful around them, my young friend." No further details about the two men were provided, and he stated the warning just once. Graves monitors carefully what words he gives up, and for better or for worse, the creeps Culp and Clifton were his employees too. For awhile, anyway.

I had heard, however, more detailed stories and warnings about them over the years, from people not guarding the truth so carefully. Most significantly, from migrants who in the past came to this area periodically, for harvesting greens and seeds from trees and similar, like we did. Some of these migrants had lost people from their group, and described the Culp and Clifton duo as the killers of the victims. Killed both by ambush and by betrayal. People from two different groups, in two separate seasons, had been shot in the back and killed. For their food and possessions, the stories went.

That was enough information for me. No proof, of

course, but I was pretty sure Culp and Clifton were the culprits. I'd seen plenty of it since humanity had capsized and went crazy, but Culp and Clifton were worse than many other villains. Because they were in our midst. And they lived here all year. They knew where to hide, where to sneak-attack from, and they were some of the very few around who always had rifles. And they'd most likely had plenty of exposure to guns, even before the Apocalypse had descended.

My trio always had weapons too, and that was most likely why we hadn't been attacked by them. Those kinds of creeps always seem to go for the helpless, the low-hanging fruit you could say. For unarmed targets, or people who'd secured guns but had no idea how to use them.

Other tales, in particular of kidnapping and sex slaves, related to Culp and Clifton may or may not have really happened. They sounded pretty awful if true. Anyway…

Amid a clear, crisp morning, with the northwest wind delivering a chilly caress but plenty of clean, fresh smells, Amos Culp and Kevin Clifton approached us. Talk about a contrast to clean, fresh smells in the air.

The tall, big-boned Culp plodded along in our direction. Pinched face with beady little pig eyes looking out from it. He'd lost a lot of weight since I'd first seen him, a few years back. He had that look of a formerly obese person who'd lost weight, fast, but had not replaced it with any added health enhancements. No alertness, vitality, or energy to go along with the trimmer persona. No sharper image brought into play, like the urge to bathe or wash up, if what I could see at that point told the truth. Especially not that oily, stringy hair of his. Keeping oneself clean is not that hard, not even in today's collapsed world. Any amount of usable water and a rag or two and you can get it done. Soap helps, but it's not critical. What excuse did this idiot in front of us have, with his undeservedly proud, leering gaze? Looking us over as if he was some kind of top dog, passing his judgment on us. With his unkempt, soiled face. The breeze blew from the two men over to our location; it wasn't long before we could actually smell Culp on top of it all.

In any case, he didn't deserve much credit for weight loss in the current day. Presently it's not that difficult to get down in weight, with a shortage of food in the post-Apocalypse and all. Although it was hard to say how much doing without Culp suffered, as it was commonly said he and his partner stole plenty of food from other people. He was just a big slug, albeit a little bit lighter weight slug that day. In my opinion, Culp didn't look dangerous or capable; no wonder he shot people in the back.

In contrast, the smaller Kevin Clifton looked squeaky clean. He was slim with streamlined muscles, maybe as a holdover from his military days, if they'd actually existed; or perhaps from hauling his equipment over miles and miles as a short-range nomad, scrambling for food. And running from attackers. Whatever he'd done had worked for him, nonetheless. Of course, he had those hollow cheekbones of the naturally slim, so maybe it was all just genetics. The kind of person who, if overeating, gains little fat and simply acquires stronger muscles. Sometimes good things happen to bad people.

Scrubbed thoroughly, yes. But Clifton, somehow, still looked unclean. Morally, I guess. He was sizing us up with sleazy eyes, the kind of eyes that promise cooperation and backstab you in turn. Looked like a slimy liar, a lifelong one. And probably good at it. I'd known tons of them in my short life. Two-faced smooth talkers. Big Army hero? Maybe. But who knew with guys like that?

Both men looked about 40, but hard to tell. Clifton's appearance, unfortunately, conveyed the impression of someone able and fit despite his years. Youthful. Bummer. Culp, in contrast, had a look that suggested a person much more tired than his chronological age should warrant. Maybe from guilt pangs eating away at him constantly. Based on the stuff I'd heard about these guys, it sounded like he could use some heavy guilt to slow up his debauchery.

On the way over to meet them we remained alert and cautious, keeping an eye out for zombie wanderers. But I wasn't too scared, not of zombies anyway. If more appeared, we'd dispatch them just like we'd done with so many in the past. No problem. Cocky? Maybe. I've wasted so many zombies at this point in my life I had reason to be.

I was on edge, however, about Amos Culp and Kevin Clifton. We knew they both carried rifles…semi-autos, in .22 caliber, to their credit. Little, accurate, copious bullets that you could find in collapsed neighborhoods and stores in boxes of 500, in the past at least. Very smart to choose such a weapon, and a choice I'd passed up to tote more firepower. As in the shotgun. Not sure as the years rolled on that I'd made the correct choice. But, almost any .22 ammo that had once been around was long gone now. Plus, how would a person reload such a small brass casing with powder and a new lead slug? I've never worked on any ammo that tiny, and I had the reloading of a much bigger shotgun shell down to a science.

Long story short: we were afraid of being sniped, shot from a spot amongst all the trees and weeds around us, as we walked to the meeting. By the very two scoundrels we were to work with. Why they would outright murder us, I had no idea. Just to take our stuff? Eliminate their competition? There's no telling what motivates unsavory characters.

But we hadn't been shot at; not yet, anyway. And so all of us, five people total, met amongst a massive stand of oak trees a mile from the mansion. Brought together to do a harvest for Mortimer Graves, in the hopes of ending up with a nice supply of food as payment. Yep, Culp and Clifton were our "help" today. Help. I doubted that they'd be very helpful, and it would turn out I was right.

If I could have run things as planned, we could have all extracted a massive bounty of acorns from the surrounding oak groves. The acorn crop was copious, and our haul could have been huge. If we'd cooperated as a team. Big if.

Were we willing to work with them? Yes. Mainly because Graves said so. Happy to see them? Hell no. That feeling was verified as correct, not long into the day. It turned out they weren't into the whole work thing that much.

When they did actually do work for Mr. Graves, they brought in harvests of seeds, maple sap, and similar, just like my ladies and I did. Compared to our gatherings, they submitted smaller harvests of all those items, yet they wanted payments equal to ours each time. They argued with Graves over the bartering as a matter of course. Not Mortimer Graves' thing at all – he liked being in charge – but he mostly put up with it. They'd never gathered acorns, and as I look back on the big picture now, it was clear that to them the nuts from the oak trees were chump change.

Once again, the two creeps brought something else to the table, something valuable. Contributions that my trio had no idea about producing or finding. Contributions that made Mr. Graves continue to associate with them, despite their obviously untrustworthy natures.

Before we came over to meet the two guys, the ladies had been informed about the facts. About the dangers, and also about the rationale as to why we were going on the outing regardless. I didn't like having to admit I simply had caved in to Graves. We needed more food, and we certainly needed the fuel to get down to Texas. But giving in proved I was his junior.

The women both seemed to think, based on their lack of reaction, that "why of course you're his junior." Money meant nothing now, but possessions and power did. They always would. And now more than ever. Mortimer Graves had both categories covered…about a billion dollars worth. And I had…what, three hundred dollars worth? But, of course, with my lady companions, I figured my life was worth a full million or so. Not a billion, but not bad.

The fact that neither Margo nor Ruby expressed any surprise toward the fact that I felt like an underling to Graves was a bit jarring. Not sure if I was to be relieved by that fact or not. I was off the hook for caving to Graves on the one hand, but…I felt smaller in a way. He was the rich, powerful guy. In contrast, was I…in actuality…but a dirt poor punk, with a handful of tools and weapons, violent urges and the skills to use them, and a slick missile of a motorcycle? Kind of like the post-Apocalypse version of a soccer hooligan? With a double barrel, ammo, and a ride?

I pondered it briefly, but didn't like that image of myself. I expunged it from my mind, and kept it out with a wall of mental resistance. Obstinate and stubborn can work wonders.

Anyway, my better halves were OK with the setup, so we proceeded. And both gals would be on red alert for danger as we all worked, weapons never far away. I was counting especially on Margo, her and her trusty shotgun. She may have been a bitch sometimes, but if needed that bitch could kill at the drop of a hat. I loved her for it.

The earth still has plenty of normal, un-transitioned humans. Some are tremendously good, hopeful, and helpful. And some are simply bad news, rotten to the core. But nearly all of them, good or bad, live their lives in fear. Because of zombies. And because of lowlives like Culp and Clifton. I wouldn't live in fear of them, but I realized the danger. I'd be watching, and ready to act defensively if needed. I expected some type of shenanigans from them, and was ready with whatever counter-strategy might be needed.

**

Culp and Clifton gathered a certain ingredient for Graves, as mentioned previously. That substance being valuable enough to represent a key ingredient in two irreplaceable potions that Graves makes. The first concoction was the derivative of penicillin I described earlier. That particular medicine the ladies and I liked to carry small doses of, in case there was a need to fight infection. Many small instances of injury occurred, all the time. Luckily, we only needed small amounts to do the job.

And that medicine we carried Culp and Clifton cared little about. They focused on the one that Graves needs to halt his regression. Without the ingredient they harvested, he'd deteriorate in due time to nothing more than one of the undead.

It seemed that they knew their value to Graves. And thus their power. They were correct. But they also thought the same power could be lorded over me. Nope.

"You two girly girls come with me," Clifton said. "We'll go to the trees down there to start. My friend Mr. Amos Culp will watch over your buddy there, while we…uh…"

Clifton stopped talking. We weren't looking at him, nor listening. I was setting up the system for the gathering and sorting of today's acorns. Accessories: three plastic buckets and a big canvas tarp. A big old aluminum cooler, probably 100 years old, that we used for about 100 different things. Two steel nutcrackers as well, to wrench the caps off the acorns. Three pairs of big trash bags, double-bagged. I kept organizing the things, studiously not looking at Culp or Clifton. The women looked at me and at what I was doing, also avoiding any eye contact with the other two men.

I secured a couple of items, and while sitting on the old cooler with the tarp across my lap, I finally looked up at the two bozos.

"So, yeah…" Clifton began, a smile of mischief creeping onto his face. Already.

"You boys lean your rifles against that tree right there," I said.

"We're good," Culp said.

"We'll see, won't we? Lean them against the tree," I said. "You planning to knock down acorns with them?"

They leaned their guns against the closest oak tree, a massive beauty with a mountain of branches above its trunk. Its acorns alone would have fed any one of us for most of the winter. Both men were looking at me with cool expressions. As if going along with what I'd said about setting down the rifles was only done because they wanted to, not because I said so. Willing to cooperate for now. But not for long.

"You were an Army Ranger or something, weren't you?" I said to Clifton. I didn't look at Culp.

"Something like that, yeah."

"So you can climb up phone poles, up ropes, stuff like that?" I said.

"Of course. You should've saw me rappel during an op over in—" he began.

"Then start climbing. You're going to be our upper branch guy. Some of the best nuts are way up there. We need 'em knocked down," I said. "The ladies here will alternate as the gatherers down below. Fling 'em down, they'll collect 'em."

"How am I supposed to get way out on the skinniest limbs? Think I'm Spider Man or something?"

"Or something. Grab a stick off the ground and carry it up with you. Do whatever works. Hey, I know enough to improvise like that, and I wasn't even a Delta Force commando," I said. Clifton glowered at me. I held his gaze.

"Why won't they both be down below the tree, collecting," Clifton said. "I thought we were trying to be as productive as possible."

"Because while one gathers, the other will be helping me sort the harvest, all the while cradling a gun. And watching the both of you," I said.

Clifton didn't like it. Not the type of scenario he expected, I believe. If he'd wanted pushovers, he'd chosen the wrong trio.

"So they'll be standing around down here, picking up some weightless nuts, or watching us and thinking about shooting us. While I, alone, have to go up in the trees and do all the risky, difficult work?" Clifton said.

"Are we to expect him to be the climbing guy?" I said, finally looking at Culp. I let my eyes wander to his midsection. It looked soft, although not that oversized. But in a chess game like this, you have to position the bishops and knights to your advantage.

"Let me tell you about my man Amos here. He can do most everything, hiking, fighting, defending what's right. And he can climb with the best of them," Clifton said.

"He might break some of the heavy branches, much less the more narrow ones," I said.

"Hey," Culp said. I ignored him. Out of the corner of my eye, I saw him look down to his waist area, then run a hand along his belly, then onto his waist, evaluating the density of the fat stores there.

"You'll be sitting around down here on the cooler, in the meanwhile?" Clifton asked.

"Yep. And directing the overall operation. Keep you guys on your toes."

"Don't overexert yourself."

"I won't. Also, I'll be removing the cap off of every acorn we harvest. Nature nearly sticks them on with Super Glue. Takes force to wrench them off, and lots of practice," I said. "Ever popped caps off of acorns, Clifton?"

Clifton didn't answer, instead looking at Culp. Deciding what to do next, not happy about things. About me.

"Wanna try? In about 20 minutes you won't be able to feel your hand or forearm muscles, the integrity of the acorn is that tough," I said. "And we have buckets of them to collect and process. Up for that?"

More silence, sarcastic looks from both dudes. But no action.

"I thought not. Look, I'm a lot more knowledgeable in this area than you two," I said. "Don't fight it."

They turned away, took a few steps, mumbling to

each other in clandestine fashion.

"I have great hearing too," I added, pretending I was on to what they'd just said. I actually had no idea, hearing nothing but murmurs. My hearing is not especially acute. Rather, it's about average. And slightly below average when Margo is complaining.

They finally turned back, looking no happier than a moment ago.

"Grab a set of trash bags, and pick up any acorns which have already dropped," I said to Culp. "Cover the whole oak stand. Start wherever you want."

Culp just looked at me, not moving. It was clear his "top dog" act from earlier wasn't going to fly today.

"Hop to," I said.

Culp looked down at the ground, shaking his head in theatrical disbelief. Like the wise old teacher about to give the young smart aleck student a serious talking to.

"Who you exactly fancying yourself to be, mister?" Culp said. He started lumbering towards me, long, large legs absent of any real athleticism. One of those bullies who had gotten by with his pushy ways most of his life, due solely to size.

"You musta been popular with the babes back in high school," Culp said. "I can see the temptation they might have felt." Yikes. A compliment from Culp. Be still, my beating heart. He moved closer.

"Amos, just a sec," Clifton said. Trying to pull Culp back. Not like Clifton was some kind of good guy. I think he wanted to execute a sneakier plan, other than Culp just strolling up to me and getting in my face.

"Like an adorable blond beach bunny, the hotshot pretty boy," Culp said, now only six feet away. Sporting his pig-like face and body odor, Culp got right in front of me. He then reached out a hand to tousle my shaggy head of hair. Probably an indulgence he'd learned years back, when working as a cop, or perhaps as a prison guard, or maybe while serving as an inmate for all I know.

Reaching. To make contact. With me. With that grubby hand.

His motion stopped. As did his grubby hand, two inches short of my hair. His eyes met mine, surprise showing in his, satisfaction in mine.

Both testicles under his filthy jeans had a shotgun barrel resting against them. Loaded barrels? Oh yeah. I'd had the double barrel resting under the tarp. Just in case. You never know who's going to get the drop on you. The disgusting doorknob Culp was maybe feeling the same way at that very moment. At times you can even get beat by a hotshot pretty boy, one as adorable as a blonde beach bunny. You just never know.

Safe to conclude, he'd never fully heard the details about Trick Chasseur. Mess up my hair, you big ox? That's for my ladies only. I nudged the barrels a little more firmly against the dunce's nuts. He backed off. Looked at me once more, did a contrived snort as if he wasn't flustered, and went back to Clifton. Good choice, slug.

Uncomfortable silence. Clifton letting his eyes wander about, checking where the women were, considering things. These guys hadn't shown up to work. They'd never intended to.

"This is bullshit," Culp said. Looking around at all of us like Clifton had done, then at the collection receptacles we had.

"How so?" I said.

He was clearly stalling. "Don't see what the point of all this is. I thought the typical acorn harvest yielded more than this," Culp said. "A few bags? Three buckets? That's looking like all we'll get. I thought there'd be a lot more."

"You thought?"

"That's what we wuz told."

"How many acorn harvests have you done?" I said.

He didn't reply, knowing where this was going. He'd completed zero acorn harvests, I'd completed many.

"Keep your spirits up, get busy and gather some. Those bags aren't getting full with you just standing there philosophizing about it all," I said. Although I knew he wouldn't collect a single acorn. He was trying to buy time with the griping.

Culp looked at me, trying to appear fearsome. I thought he might start jumping up and down, stomping his feet. In frustration of course; he probably wanted to kill me, but found out it may not be so easy. He'd certainly discovered the close contact intimidation approach was a very bad idea. And if he and Clifton lunged for their guns, at this point we had them covered. Neither of the guys held a gun, all three of us did.

"Unless you fellas didn't actually show up to do any work at all today. Unless this meeting was…intended for something else."

I never did find out what their ultimate plan had been. A typical gathering of an acorn harvest for my trio was four, five, maybe six hours. Depended on the availability of the crop, how much daylight we had, and if we were attacked by zombies or not. Culp wouldn't last two hours doing harvest work by the look of him. Maybe not even one hour. These guys were thieves and killers, not laborers. I'd known it all along. What final goal did they hope to achieve?

No way to know for sure. But my suspicion was that they were going to ransack us, somehow. But to what end? Abscond with our equipment? Didn't make sense. You could find tools and receptacles like we had anywhere. No money to take, like in the old days. Not the nuts from the harvest…we hadn't gathered any yet.

In brief flashes of clarity as this whole pathetic scene was unfolding, I saw an unnerving possibility. The first thing Clifton wanted to do with our group was separate the women from me. To do this while Culp stood around, not appearing to be ready for work in any way. Standing around, doing nothing but cradling a rifle. Readying for something else perhaps?

Wild guess: Clifton leads them away to start a food gathering project he knows nothing about. Wait until both women set their weapons down, Clifton scoops the guns up. Culp then takes me out (good luck with that). The scumbags proceed to abduct the women. Too horrifying to think about.

"You're not up for this kind of rigor, Culp. And you know it. And Mr. Special Forces over there," I said. "Seems to me he'll do whatever he can to get out of an honest day's work."

"OK, I've had enough from this disrespectful, babyfaced dip. The bossman wannabe," Clifton said. He approached, squaring off, about 15 feet back from where I sat on the old aluminum cooler. His hand went down to the handle of a big sheath knife, still in its case and tucked down into the side of his waistband.

"We'll see who's king of the hill," Clifton said.

"This is mostly wetland around here. Not many hills," I said.

Touché.

"You know what I mean," Clifton stammered. "Heard you think you're good with a knife."

"That is the case, in fact. But primarily for filleting rabbits and fish," I said.

"Yeah? How about you draw one of those blades, and stand up and face someone your own size. We'll settle this for real."

"Is that right?" I said. "It's about to get real?"

"I believe I'd make it so, young fella." Clifton took another step forward, continuing to clutch the handle of his still-sheathed knife.

"You know what I think?"

"What, pretty boy?" Clifton said.

"I think you'd look pretty funny trying to engage in a knife fight with half your head gone," I said. I glanced to my left, to where Margo had braced against a big oak trunk. Her 20-gauge's muzzle was pointed directly at Clifton.

Outstanding. Ah, Margo. She overreacted sometimes. Could result in problems. But most of the time, I kind of thought it was cool. Not waiting to see if the challenge from Clifton resolved itself, or petered out. No. Instead, draw a bead on the threat with a loaded shotgun, then click off the safety.

Some people, upon first seeing Margo, might have concluded that she was like one of the shapely, giggly cheerleaders in high school. When in reality, she was one of the more explosive women, as attractive as the cheerleader ditz but with four times the strength. She was that one on the volleyball team, the best spiker, the one who specialized in bursting the ball down onto the bridge of the nose of her opponent. Trick Chasseur was definitely not the only badass in our trio. If we were stone cold killers, like I suspected the dweebs in our presence of being, it would have been curtains for Kevin Clifton.

"This is between the two of us. For us to work out," Clifton said. He tried to be cool about it, but also seemed like he was waiting for the blast from Margo's gun to meet his temple.

I said nothing. Margo said nothing, and the bead on

her shotgun didn't waver. Ruby said nothing, per usual. But glancing over, I found something surprising. And pleasing. Culp had taken a moment to look up from his waistline and focus on something else. He realized he was in the sights of Ruby's rifle. She sat cross-legged, at ease, the lever action cowboy gun ready to blast off if violence erupted. Thatta girl. Man, I loved the babes I was stuck with.

"Just us," Clifton said, his voice quivering.

I said nothing.

"It's not for blondie over there to interfere with," Clifton said, continuing the theme. "She better watch herself, or one day, hopefully soon, me and my partner just might drag her and her brunette friend off into the brush. Why, we'd–"

I saw a little red, a microsecond of white hot, and the muzzle of my double barrel was suddenly flush against Clifton's cheek. It had hit with a popping sound, the impact of the steel pushing past rubbery cheek flesh to the bone beneath. No cutting, just a serious smack.

I didn't remember the lunge up and away from my sitting place on the cooler, but sparks of anger could make me jettison into action, as if lit up by some of Graves' nitro-enriched fuel.

"What will you do? C'mon, say it," I said.

"You'll be sorry, you clueless little shithead."

"Say it, Mr. Green Beret. Say it. I dare you." I pressed the barrels into his cheek a little more. "Threatening me is one thing, but–," I started to say.

He tried to swipe the barrels away. I gotta admit, that took guts. I moved the shotgun's steel tubes-of-death back, let his swipe swish in the air, then slammed the barrels into the top of his chest. Enough to bruise, I'm sure. He huffed in pain, got his footing back, then faced me again.

"Here's what we do, you arrogant punk. No weapons," he said. "To the knockout. Or to the death if I feel like it." He slipped the sheath and its knife from his waistband, dropping them to the ground.

"Forget it. I'd rather not waste the energy. We've got acorns to harvest. Only so many hours in a day," I said. "I'm sure you understand, soldier boy."

Why did I have to add that last part? I always have to provoke. So foolish. But there is a little sadistic joy in it, I have to admit.

"No. It's go time," Clifton said, his face contorting into a grimace.

I never agreed to it. Matter of fact, if he was a better man, I would have warned him. But it wasn't to be. No, Clifton was bent on a fistfight.

He closed the distance between us, feinted forward, pulled back, ready for the charge with both fists down by his waist. Lunged forward, predictably. Straight from the U.S. Army Infantry self-defense manual. As outdated as it was. He even put his head down a little, like a charging bull in the cartoons. Which actually helped me.

One kick. A tight roundhouse. A motion I'd done 12,000 times, minimum. Thumped right behind Clifton's ear, smashing him down to the grassy ground. Probably felt like a sledgehammer coated in a leather boot. He started to rise up, then went back down to all fours, concentrating on the grass for a moment. Probably seeing three different versions of the grass blades swimming in his vision.

He was going to choose me for a weaponless fight? Oh, Clifton. You flex on me? Don't be silly.

"Should we call it a day?" I offered. I was pretty sure he was going to pick up and draw his fighting knife next. If so, then it was goodnight, Clifton. The opinion of Graves be damned. I was still holding my shotgun, by the way. Yep, draw your blade, Clifton, and I'll cut you in half.

But no. Clifton got up, tottered a little, then looked for his knife on the ground. Found it, stuffed it back down into his waistband. He looked at me, didn't really seem to recognize who I was, then started walking away. Slowly.

Culp slowly grabbed both rifles...Margo and I both took an extra step toward him, the beads of both of our shotguns on that gathering of flesh in Culp's center. Culp knew it...he cradled the guns, not ready to shoot in any way. Smart move, meathead.

That pair of winners, Culp and Clifton, disappeared into the swampland, tails between their legs.

***

That was sure a mess.

The two rejects were gone for now, and we had to get to work.

We decided to have one of us sit out at all times, gun in hand, watching the section of swamp into which the two weasels had stumbled away. And to the left of it, and right of it. Listening for disturbances, for splashes of swamp water, for twigs breaking. We didn't feel like suffering a .22 caliber ambush.

A massive haul of acorns may have been chump change to the morons we'd just chased away, but to us, it was like manna from heaven. The collection of the nuts was elementary for my trio, having the system down so well by that point in time. And no, we didn't climb up any oak trees. That's what my pole pruner was for. I extended it, maneuvered it up high, tapping certain branches and chopping off others as needed. Acorns fell by the pound, and quickly. Stupid Clifton had actually thought I was serious about him playing Spider Monkey up in the thin branches. He was supposed to be a commando of some sort?

We had every receptacle filled shortly after we started. This is what we could have done with a couple of trusted helpers, but even more quickly, and the total would have been even more fruitful.

The sleazebags Culp and Clifton had other ideas. Seemingly devious ones. It may have meant the death of all three of us, for all we knew.

The double-cross by Culp and Clifton was anticipated and thwarted, however. Sadly, we hadn't seen the last of the degenerates. They'd appear again in our future. And then, well, things would get really brutal.

And the whole Culp and Clifton experience threw us off. Time wasted. Well, not fully, when you think about it. Ruby got another much-needed real life drill on taking aim and preparing to kill. For when it really mattered. For Margo, she did what she already excelled at, but practice keeps it all sharp.

As for me, I got to go into my ball-busting act, in earnest. I really savored those moments. And I got one really solid, satisfying kick in. Just like the old days. Connecting on a dufus's head right where the ear region ends and the base of the skull begins. A natural depression resides there, making a nice spot to catch and focus all of a strike's force.

Oh, why did moments like that have to pass? Guns at the ready, lethal babes at my side, my poison-tipped tongue in top form, and skull-thumping martial arts. Vanquishing the enemy. It was wrong, but how I felt at that moment: current day living sucks in a way, but if there's an almighty authority up there listening…you may penalize me or whatever, but I have to request it.

Please don't let the post-Apocalypse end. We lived in horror sometimes, but other moments I'd have never traded for anything.

Good times, good times.

10

Soon after, on a tip from the Minnow Man, the ladies and I went fishing.

We rode our cycles to a fishing hotspot he'd described: Wild Rice Creek, where it deepened from its usual two feet down to six. A ton of edible fish, in this case perch, were congregating here in prep for their fall run to the much deeper Green Weed Pond, downstream just a ways.

After Horace the Minnow Man told us about it, we knew we'd go. Fresh fish fried up with herbs and acorn butter sounded tremendous. Our commute was to a section of the creek nearly three miles from the mansion. It was down the old freeway, that particular stretch mostly free of debris, and thus an easy cycle ride. Compared to hiking, it was faster and safer to use the cycles. Plus, the machines needed to be put through their paces once in a while.

So in the late morning on that sunny 79-degree day, we set off to the creek to capture some perch. And if that worked out, immerse ourselves in the chilly waters once done.

We weren't fishing with rods, reels, hooks, and line, as I'd often done since boyhood. Instead, we were using a flexible net – known by anglers as a seine – that could be walked through the water. If successfully done, it would envelope a whole handful of fish at a time. Much more effective than a hook and line. Sometimes. The seine had been left for our usage in the barn by the Minnow Man himself. Graves had come up with the materials for a brand new fishing seine, and after handing it off to Mr. Minnow, a brand new, much better seine was soon woven together for his harvesting duties. Graves directed the Minnow Man to give us the old beat-up one. No complaints here; the price was right. I took off the old handles and put a five-foot tree branch on either side of the old net. With two people, you could hold up either side of the net with those long branches, and form a capturing swath in the water nearly seven feet wide. Like a spider web for minnows.

Once at Wild Rice Creek, we stripped to our underwear and waded in, the sun starting to lovingly bake our exposed skin. Even in the age of the Apocalypse, a person needs Vitamin D. Our half-naked hunt for fish was hopefully doing double duty: a meal and a tan.

At about three feet deep, we started seeing the perch, most of the fish about six inches long, some longer, some shorter. They saw us too, darting backward in the creek, away from us, and forward, to us, and to our right and left. Frantic. Which would work for our purposes.

The strategy in brief: the sight of us moving in the water sent the little tasty fish swimming in alarm; holding still, in contrast, didn't scare them much. So…the ladies posted with the net, one holding each side. Standing motionless in the water, the seine blocking almost half the width of the creek. Trick, stealthy perch hunter that he is, started down the creek from them about 20 yards or so, where the water was nearly five feet deep. Slowly stepping forward, to the right side of the creek, then the left, making the impression of a slow moving, unpredictable predator. One seeking little fish. The little fish didn't like it…and made their way to things not so scary. Rock piles on the bottom, fallen branches in the water, weed cover…and an unmoving net which may have looked like more weed cover.

Whoops.

Ruby and Margo lifted the net, with four healthy, colorful perch flipping about in the net's webbing. They steered the net away from the creek, and dumped the scaly prey on the grass at water's edge. Net back in the water, a repeat of the perch herding, two more fish. Another pass, three more. At just over a dozen captured, we wrapped up the fishing operation.

A small cooler, about half the size of our unit for acorn harvesting, had been attached to the back of Margo's bike. We put the fish in there with plenty of water. The water would be dumped out right before we headed back, to reduce weight. But first...

Swimming! Not something we often got a chance to do in the environment in which we lived...neither up north nor down south. So we went for it. Zombies would be atypical here, since most wandering humans wouldn't end up in an out-of-the-way creek bottom. Roads, former neighborhoods, downtowns, basically typical human haunts of yesteryear were prime hunting grounds for our zombie friends. They went where they sensed the food – in other words the people – would be. So this swimming hole looked safe, and its wetness beckoned. The water temp was fine, the current was gentle, and no poisonous snakes lived in the area. And it looked like the coast was clear.

Or so we thought.

A sense from somewhere made a tingle spark along the back of my neck. I knew – before I officially knew – something, or someone, was watching. I could feel it in the air. And yep, it was real. From the direction away from the highway, on the side of the sprawling wetland tangles, a figure's silhouette appeared up the hillock, the sun momentarily blocked as the being stepped above us on the creekside. I burst out of the water, wet undies still in place, and snatched the double barrel away from the tree stump it rested against. I heard the ladies scrambling too, going toward nearby brushy cover and the location of their own firearms. I'd just brought up the gun, looking down the barrels in order to align the bead of the boomstick with its intended target. In case said intruder needed to be my shotgun's target.

The intruder didn't need to be. I relaxed my arms, and lowered the shotgun. It was none other than the Minnow Man. Apparently making sure we found the secret perch run spot as he'd described it. At ease, inquisitive, no weapons like usual, just a small fishing satchel strapped across his shoulders, the basket itself resting by his left hand. I relaxed, placing the double-barreled shotgun back against the stump.

"It's just the Minnow Man," I said to Margo and Ruby, then looked away from our guest to the ladies. They were already looking at him. And he was looking at them. And he kept looking them. The women with nothing but their underwear bottoms on.

"Hey," I said. There was firmness to my voice, my alarm from a moment ago changing to annoyance. "You can watch me, but you can't watch them."

"I don't want to watch you," the Minnow Man said. He looked over at Margo, her slim body and white butt scrambling from the creek, to Ruby who was already out, handing her a handful of garments. The Minnow Man was entranced.

"Look at me, not them, Horace," I said, as calm as I could. He ignored me. Then I went theatrical, speaking as if through a megaphone. Kind of like on the old cop shows.

"Horace the Minnow Man," I bellowed, as close to an electronic voice as I could get. As close as I could remember to what it sounded like in the movies and on TV.

"Look away from the women." Saying *away* like *ah-waayyyy*, with emphasis on it like the cop actors did in the shows. I tried to be cool about it, and I didn't want to be too aggressive. I know he went without, probably forever for all I knew. He was our ally. But this oddball geek had to be reined in. The Minnow Man looked at me as I'd commanded, the desire in his eyes gone, now clearly frightened. I could kill him in three seconds, and he knew it.

"You scare them. You can't do that. I won't allow it," I said.

"Well, Mr. Graves considers me a full-fledged employee. They are but your subcontractors, as far as he's concerned. I rank higher. Just ask Mr. Graves."

"To hell with Mortimer Graves."

He looked back as if shocked by a cattle prod.

"This doesn't concern directives from him, it concerns instructions from me. I know you desire a woman. What guy doesn't? But you're talking about my whole world here," I said, motioning my head toward the women.

"I guess I am, aren't I? But, you know, Kittrick…"
How did he know that?

"Trick."

"Uh, yeah, Trick. Sorry…"

"Don't be. Just talk and stop apologizing," I said to the Minnow Man.

"I've never been with a woman. You see, the whole world went topsy-turvy when people started turning into zombies and decaying and everything."

"I've gathered as much," I said. Oh man, had I gathered it.

"I've not touched one. A woman. Ever. I was just starting college when…"

So he and I were similar in age. This little, capable

guy in front of me had some hard years on him. Holy smokes. I pegged him at 36, 38, maybe even 40. The wear and tear he showed was proof that a decent zombie Apocalypse can add 10 years, minimum.

Had women been helping to keep me young? Physically, it couldn't hurt. Psychologically, well…I could write a book. If you're a guy, you know. Back to the Minnow Man:

"And women haven't responded how I'd hoped. I've helped several as they've come through, all alone, or with a group. Sometimes with some dumbass guy of some kind. I'd always hoped they'd discard the guy and choose me. You know, because of my cave making skills. My fish harvesting skills. You know. What do you think?" the Minnow Man rambled.

"I think you smell like fish," I replied. I looked him square in the eye. He knew I meant it…literally.

"I…smell like fish?" the Minnow Man said.

I nodded, glancing at Ruby, who had her clothes on fully, and at Margo, who had only her bra and jeans on. She'd picked up her shotgun to ready position. I shook my head no at her. I looked back to him; the Minnow Man was staring at her. He didn't seem to care about her gun.

"Me," I said. "Look at me."

He turned suddenly back in my direction, looking my direction as if surprised I was still there.

"Yeah, that bad fish odor thing. Hmm," he said. "I wasn't aware."

"You're probably too used to it to know. But it could factor in, as far as rejection," I said. "The bathing routine, once you get into it…"

"Bathing? Oh, but I do," the Minnow Man said. "I bathe in this creek, a couple of other ones nearby, and in Green Weed Pond. At least every other day. Full body, and my hair gets rinsed as I dive for my minnow traps."

"Well…" I said, seriously wondering how the fish smell could accumulate on him like it did. Then it occurred to me. What if…

"So earlier today, you met up with Mr. Graves for a trade of some kind, I'm guessing," I said.

"Yes. I'd secured seven perch of my own, just like you folks are doing. With a seining net stretched across the creek, like you used. Less than a mile from here," the Minnow Man said.

"And those are going to be for Graves' food supply?" I said.

"Uh, in this case, just the heads. He had me separate the heads from the bodies, and took those with some of the entrails. He's going to use those ingredients in one of his grinders. Making dog food for that giant mutt of his."

I looked into his eyes for a second before saying the next part.

"And what did you do…with the rest of the fish bodies?"

"Oh. I have them right here. In my satchel," he said, touching the basket on his hip.

I grinned at him, restraining the smile at first. As I thought about dead fish, butchered ones no less, in the hot sun, riding in a non-insulated container on his person…perhaps for hours…my smile grew broader. Partly to kid him a little, and partly as an expression of my disbelief. Not just toward him, but to the way life was shaking out. This freaky little swamp crawler in front of us was one of our only remaining compatriots in the world. I couldn't get the smile to go away, perhaps because of what felt like approaching insanity. Or similar.

The Minnow Man looked stunned as he put it all together, an *Oh Wow* look on his face, seeming to show some appreciation for the enlightenment, as his nimble hand went to the fish basket. I nodded once to him then turned to rejoin my partners; we gathered our things, including our cooler of fish. As we started our exit, it did occur to me, again, that in a world of unfriendlies, that weirdo was one of our few trusted neighbors. Had to remember that. Before we maneuvered through the greenery to our cycles, I glanced back to him one more time, to wave goodbye and neutralize any hard feelings.

The Minnow Man had already disappeared without a trace into the brush.

11

Freshly caught and gently fried fish now filled our stomachs. I could almost feel the protein working its way into exhausted muscles, speeding the body's recovery and soothing the brain.

The perch that had ended up in our net, the very ones swimming in Wild Rice Creek just that morning, were now history. A bit of slicing, dicing, and tactical filleting, and we had a whole pan full of little perch steaks.

We'd also lucked out by discovering a couple of clumps of wild chives growing near the creek. Before we left to head back to our living quarters, I grabbed a handful. That collection of herbs also ended up cut into pieces and dropped into the pan. A layer of warmed acorn butter awaited the chives, and with the addition of a cupful of pine nuts, we had an excellent batter for blanketing the fish fillets.

The heads and innards of the fish had been secured in a plastic bag and deposited into a little freezer Graves supplies for us. We'd turn them over to him, and those fish parts would go into a processor of some kind in the mansion. Combined with other ingredients, the fish leftovers would end up as tasty dog pebbles for Helmut's food dish. Heh, just like the Minnow Man, we helped keep that big ornery dog alive with our contributions of fish and game leftovers. And what appreciation did we receive from the animal? A giant, irate face with the body of a rhinoceros behind it staring at us. Like we were its next chicken drumstick. That kind of appreciation. But I'm getting off the beaten track here.

Ah, yes, plenty of chow. And as good as the fish and buttery acorn sauce were, there was more. Dessert. Dessert! You may have doubted the complete truth of my tale earlier, but now you might be thinking: what kind of supposed post-Apocalypse experience is this guy relaying? Dessert? Why isn't it like the Apocalypse the rest of us lived through?

Because, my friends, you didn't have Mortimer Graves as your food preparer. He may have been half-zombie, but he was all chef. Case in point:

Take a pile of wild plums. Then mix up a batch of clover flower petals with super sweet maple syrup. Add some herbs from the field for the slightest spice. Cover said plums with the syrupy concoction, then bake them for about an hour on low heat. The syrup is heated up and seals onto the already sweet plums as a golden glaze. It actually flakes off as you stick the fork or your teeth into it, the crumbles as tasty as any brown sugar you've ever consumed.

Yes, the beauty of resourcefulness in the post-Apocalypse.

The distribution breakdown of glazed plums was five for Margo, five for Ruby, and six for me. I'm larger and my charisma is more intense, so I generally get the extra serving.

In this case, before eating my portion, I had to tend to the guns, cleaning them and making sure all adjustments were on the mark. We were heading out soon, and didn't want any snafus on the road. Meanwhile, the lovely ladies feasted on their plums. The rigors of our schedule and the sudden infusion of carbohydrates into their system apparently helped the women drift off to sleep soon after.

There was so much to think about, to worry about if I had been that kind of person, with our departure from Minnesota and subsequent trip to Texas. It was right ahead of us now. A million ways to die, to be killed. None would befall us though, if my plans went through as usual. It would all work out. Just like the sugary plums I was inspecting at the time would. On the little fancy plate in front of me, the china piece a discard from Graves' illustrious collection, as was the elegant fork I held. One from Belgium, the other from Austria. So upscale, suitable for a finely prepared, sweet dessert. Just a single lamp was on in the barn, the lighting therefore nice and subdued, both of my partners nourished and resting. Just Trick with his fork and his plums, about to put no less than six of them down the hatch. I moved the pointy fork prongs to the first glazed plum, anticipating sugary goodness.

From outside came unwelcome noise. Yelling. Scolding. Growling. Then a gun shot. Then another. All coming from the direction of the Graves Mansion.

I was so fatigued. I didn't need the disruption. The uncertainty. The peril.

And worst of all, the ruckus had disturbed the enjoyment of my sugary dessert.

Somebody was gonna die.

***

I grabbed my loaded double barrel 12-gauge from its resting spot, plus four extra shells, then moved across the barn. I opened the locked door and stepped outside. With no hesitation, I shut and secured the door even before my eyes adjusted to the dark; this was a moment of danger, coming out of a lighted area into the blackness of night. But if an attacker waited for me, getting me before my eyes adjusted to the dark, well, so be it. I didn't want the ladies to suffer it as well. Sugary desserts or not, this zombie land living isn't that simple.

Would the gals inside be in shock? Stunned? Terrified at my sudden departure? No. As instructed, they'd then grab their own weapons and proceed to sit tight. Inside, secured, protecting the home front. If I got murdered out there while all alone, well, tough luck. I'd insisted to both of them: put yourself first. If you can save me, great. But a sure way to get all three of us killed off was to rush out into an unsure situation, running hither and yon, right into the clutches or rifle sights of the enemy. I would have bet anything that once disturbed and realizing I'd scrambled into the dark night, they arose from their beds, picked up their guns, and hunkered down. They knew what to do. If their boyfriend returned, let him back in. If not, carry on with life as best possible without him. I've heard that said boyfriend was an arrogant jerk anyway.

***

So as things progressed that night, I didn't end up dying. Instead, I approached the mansion unimpeded in the dark. But not really paying much attention to the big castle at all as I advanced. Instead, I made lots of pauses, looking slowly to the right and left, listening behind me, peering ahead to see if anyone, or anything, was crouched and waiting in the direction I was going. Caution is the better part of valor, after all. I saw nothing significant, not then anyway.

A slam of some kind reverberated from near the mansion. Could have been the front gate, probably was. Except Graves normally closed it with great care, showing his gentility and making a production of how amazing that entrance point to his grounds was. Quite proud of all his mansion's features, including the property and the electrified iron fence surrounding it.

And its heavy gate. He'd guide it shut gradually, or even use his handy remote control, which would close the opening even more slowly. Things surrounding the situation were feeling off just about then.

I heard voices in the dark, to my right, maybe 60 or 70 feet away. Where the grassland led to the wetland – the greenery turning thick and swampy. The density of the weeds and trees there making a great place to retreat to, if escape was necessary. Which seemed possible for the owners of those voices, after the occurrence of yelling, slamming…and shooting. Angry voices. Male. More than one. Most likely two. I had a good guess which two.

But I could see no one over there, with the area near the fading sounds completely dark. Nobody was to be seen near Graves' slightly illuminated grounds either. I got up near the gate of the mansion finally, my shotgun at the ready. As were my legs…in case I had to sprint the hell out of there. I was met only by silence. Then – *whoosh*!

Helmut rushed the gate, fangs alight, eyes ablaze. Froth flew from his jaws as he snapped over and over again near the bars of the gate; I could have sworn I saw some blood droplets fly amongst the rest of the foam. The pissed off canine's attack burst the silence: loud, mesmerizing, stunning, all at once. The intensity shook even me. For crying out loud, I'd hate to be that thing's chew toy. Thank heavens the damn gate was closed.

"Hey!" I shouted. "It's me, you numbskull."

His growls became less intense, sinking down to more of a terrible hum, once seeing me clearly, hearing my familiar voice. It was an improvement. He may not have liked me much, but I had worked for his master for several summers, stopping by the compound regularly and repeatedly. Heck, I lived on the same property that the dog did, more or less.

"You should know me by this time," I said, my voice now at normal volume. But he had to keep grumbling, the angry eye thing continuing, as if to save face. I ignored the dog then, letting my eyes search for anything out of place…anything in motion. Besides Helmut's animated twitching, of course.

Motion straight ahead, from inside the fenced area, beyond the Helmut mountain of flesh and aggression. Ah. None other than the man himself, Mr. Graves. He strode from the left side of the mansion, at ease. But not looking particularly happy. His suit was in place, rumpled but still looking top quality; no bow tie in place, uncharacteristically. As if Graves had been settling in for the evening, probably about to switch into his comfy robe or whatever he wore at night. He held what I assumed was a remote in his hands, larger than the usual one he carried, the one I was used to seeing. It had a glowing aqua blue light at the end, a small one, about the size of a pea. I started wondering what the device was exactly…if it wasn't simply a remote. A weapon? A laser beam thing? Some kind of gun? Never knew with Graves. I figured I better announce myself, just in case.

"It's me, Mortimer."

"Yes, Master Trick, I'm aware of that. It's dark out, but I detected your scent on the breeze," Graves said.

Detected your scent. He did? Or did he mean to say Helmut did?

"Um, yeah," I said. "Shooting. Yelling. Scrambling. Things going slam in the night. Helmut angry."

"Helmut is always angry," Graves said.

"Then the other things. What just went down over here, Mortimer?"

"A little visit. An unpleasant visit, to be exact. Our two friends from the aborted acorn collection project. As you mentioned, they weren't cooperative with you on that effort. Not particularly cooperative just now either."

"Culp and Clifton just visited, is what you're saying."

"Oh, yes."

"Gunshots. Theirs?"

"Yes. Two shots. From the larger one. The really stupid one," Graves said. The gentle lighting from his property's lamps shone on his face, ever so slightly. His eyes had a certain glimmer, a spark or something, that usually wasn't there. I pretended not to notice.

"Old Amos Culp."

"That's correct," Graves said. "He had one miss, one hit."

One hit.

"You?" I said.

"Yes. Here," Graves said, pointing to his side. I looked at the fabric of his suit. It was dark fabric, entrenched in the darkness of night, no light anywhere other than those few small lamps burning along the top of his property's fence. Couldn't see a bullet wound there at all, with the mentioned factors, plus the reality of a .22 slug's entry hole being so small. A .22 shot into a living thing can prove to make a very deadly wound, but a small entry hole nevertheless.

No wound to be seen, but near his shoe, two blood drips escaped and splashed soundlessly on the concrete patio. Then a third. Blood running down his leg. Bright red…very bright. Not a profuse stream, but blood was in fact escaping. I nodded to Graves, acknowledging the hit.

"How bad, Mortimer?"

"Not bad at all. Thanks for asking. Even for a, well, standard person, it wouldn't be that big of a deal. Went right through the skin and tagged a little muscle. A normal person would be recovered with a scar in six months. Me, well, with my current constitution…do you follow?"

"Of course. Your partially transitioned situation," I said.

"Yes. That, followed by the potent medicine I need, this little wound will be gone in a week."

"Hurt?"

"Not much," Graves said. "Although if the bullet hit me in the head, it would hurt even less. I'd be gone for good. No semi-transitioned condition or medicine can save a blown up brain."

"I suppose not," I said.

I actually knew that already. When you shoot lots and lots of zombies over the years, after awhile you pick up a few things.

Graves' eyes continued with their extra energy, that subdued glow. A fury of some kind was building up. And something else, I suspected. I didn't know what.

"The other shot? A miss?"

"Yes, I'm very happy to say. It was the second bullet he fired, hit one of the wrought iron chairs. Aimed at Helmut. Helmut was scrambling in his direction, moving fast."

"Helmut get a bite?"

"Oh, yes. Yes," Graves said. He actually looked upwards a little into the dark sky, the unhappiness fading for a second. Contentment replaced it. "Helmut sunk the fangs in pretty well, into the guy's thigh, but just for a moment. That Clifton guy was starting toward us, and Helmut flung the first one toward him. I blocked Helmut, then slammed the gate shut; Clifton was going to shoot but Culp grabbed him, pleading for help. A frantic melee, unexpected –"

"Wait. They were inside the gate?"

"Just Culp. I'd opened the gate to hand him a noodle

portion. Kind of a goodwill gesture," Graves said.

"Goodwill for what?" I wasn't following.

"They arrived here, guns in hand, to demand I give them their payment. For the harvest."

Harvest?

"As I told you, they did nothing. I think they meant to rob us, or worse. As I described to you."

"And I'm sure you are correct in that theory. They, however, were here to collect the full payment for the acorn haul," Graves said.

"They gathered none."

"Understood. Still wanted payment. In the form of food. Lots of food. Boxes of it. And a supply of medicine. They said it was the agreement."

There was no more to say about it. Culp and Clifton were ruthless, and the truth didn't matter to them. They saw an angle, and were going to exploit it. Post-Apocalypse mobster crime. Same as the old mobster crime. Strongarm. Con games. Extortion.

"You're the bedrock of the tiny economy here. Did they mean to scare you with the shooting?" I asked.

"No. To kill, once I refused. And after I gave them some seriously bad news. Culp was aiming for my heart, actually. I have some agility left. I zigged, his rifle zagged. Helmut moved, the rest of the action ran its course. Now you're here," Graves said.

"To kill you? If you're gone, they're done."

"True. And I decided to speed things up a bit, young Trick. As the conversation escalated, I made a decision. And told them, then and there. That they'd be out of all my business dealings, from now on," Graves said. "That the noodles I was handing them were a severance package of sorts."

"Are you slipping, Mortimer? No disrespect, but...you opened the gate for those bastards? When you had bad news to break? While they had guns?"

Graves didn't reply, looking off into the distance, seeming to think about it.

"Heck, even I'm talking to you through a locked gate right now," I said.

"I don't dare open it at this time, Trick. With Helmut so on edge and all."

"He looks preoccupied right now, I must say."

The dog was inspecting the ground nearby. More blood droplets. Darker than the ones dripping from Graves. Darker…and more like normal red blood. Not the brighter red as in the blood from Graves…which was so bright it was nearly neon. And that of course was not real normal. Abnormal. But I expected nothing different from my boss. In contrast, the blood Helmut was looking at…normal crimson in color…was clearly from another source.

"That from the reject known as Culp?" I said.

"Yes." Graves inspected the blood. His unhappiness from earlier continued to stay away…he was looking more at ease, the more he looked at the blood drips from Culp. The subdued glow in his eyes was becoming less subdued. More...aroused, I guess. Uh-oh.

"Mortimer," I said, more forcefully than planned. It didn't matter. He kept looking at the blood spots. "Yo!"

That got his attention. Just minutes ago, I was secure inside the barn, at our little table, sugar-coated plums in front of me. Now, I was out in the dark raising my voice. First at a giant attack dog, then at a wealthy half-zombie. Not sure my life plan was rolling out in the way I'd once envisioned.

"Yes, that leakage there is from Culp himself," Graves continued. "Not me, not my dog."

I paused a moment, as did Graves. Helmut looked up from the blood drops, curious about the silence. Saw it was nothing but a young man and old man standing there, not knowing what to say to each other. The dog looked back down at the blood, sniffing at it. Probably wishing the owner of the blood was still there for more crunching action.

"That a ray gun you're holding there?" I said. I smiled, the start of a chuckle type of thing, to let him know I was kidding. In case the gadget really was a deadly ray gun…and in case that new glow in his eyes threw off his judgment. Especially concerning who was and who wasn't the enemy.

"Oh, this," Graves said, with little concern. As in, what's one more space age device? "Transmitter for the fence's electrical charge. Just making sure the high voltage is on. Normally it's simply set to repel. A little shock to the system. Send our undead friends packing, let them expire elsewhere."

"Sure," I said.

"But just now I set the charge to maximum. Until the primary danger abates."

"Until Culp and Clifton back off," I said.

"Or die," Graves said, no jest conveyed whatsoever. The higher voltage had also spread to his eyes, by the look of it. "Now the fence's charge is set to 'kill on contact' mode. The name says it all. The top setting: Code Crispy, as I like to call it. Affectionately, of course."

"Of course," I said. I took one step back from the iron gate.

"An apt choice, young sir," Graves said. He attempted a smile, but it was almost like a subdued snarl. His eyes still contained that little extra…electricity, I guess you could say.

Time to address safety concerns, enough chitchat here. Graves had electric lamps burning at four spots on the fence near the front gate. It lit up that area of the fence, plus the dog's menacing image, part of the outline of Graves standing there…and unfortunately, me. Easy mark for a sniper in the dark. Needed to head to safety, in this case either the barn or the pitch dark.

"You seem to be in one piece, Mortimer," I said. "Nobody here for me to shoot or subdue. I better get back, close up the shutters and all."

"I'd advise the same. And I myself will do likewise. We're both partly illuminated with the light on us. Possible assailants with rifles won't be."

I glanced in the direction I'd be heading. "I've decided I have a tentative answer to your earlier question, Trick," Graves said. I looked back at him.

"I believe I opened the gate for one or both men to step in, partly to hand over that last food payment to them. But, in the back of my mind, I was hoping for more. Meeting after meeting with them seemed to be leading up to a confrontation. Tonight wasn't the first time they've threatened me. Although bullets have never flown before. I had an urge to put them both in their place, after they became hostile tonight. Nobody treats a member of the Graves family in such a manner. So I opened the gate."

"To what, lure them in?"

"Haven't decided fully. That's probably pretty close to the truth, however."

"You didn't even have one of your swords with you," I said. I smiled slightly. Only half meaning it.

"I did not, you're correct. It won't happen again," Graves said. "Next time I'll have one along." He didn't smile at all. He fully meant it.

"While we're on the subject, Trick, the offer still stands regarding one of my swords," Graves said. "In my opinion, you've earned the armament. And it goes without saying you'd put the weapon to good use. I've got a certain one picked out for you, if you decide to accept. I'd be more than pleased to equip you with one of the big blades. I can think of a couple of buffoons you could initially practice on."

"Ha. I get ya. But, as I understand it, all of your swords are collectors' editions," I said.

"Of course. Or I wouldn't own them."

"That might be a little rich for my blood, Mortimer. Thanks anyway. More of a machete man, I guess."

He nodded once, and having processed it, moved on.

"A machete will definitely work for most things. Say, before you go. Some new responsibilities for you and your lady friends have arisen. Before you head south. An important job, although not real extensive," Graves said. "Substantial pay. Up for it?"

"I'm game."

"Tomorrow, we'll discuss it. Let's plan for eleven AM." He turned on his heel, heading for the mansion, without another word or gesture. Helmut followed him. I assumed the dog was dissatisfied from the conflict earlier, with only having had a chance to sink a partial bite into Culp. But the dog trotted behind Graves with full spirit and energy, posture suggesting it was waiting to go on the attack another day...eager for it. Leading its way was that thick head full of sharp teeth and carnivorous intentions, the body carried along with the muscles of an Angus bull.

Feeling glad to not have been Amos Culp tonight, nor the owner of that leg of his that Helmut had savaged, I turned and headed back to the barn, the pitch dark awaiting me. Just as I was awaited by my lovely partners. And by a plate of sugar coated plums.

12

"You actually know the location?" I said to Mortimer Graves. Graves didn't answer right away. An old, sturdy briefcase rested on the table between us. He reached into it again, removing yet another item for me to take with. Partial payoff in advance for the last-minute assignment he was handing over to us. A "rush" order you might say, with the appropriate special fees included.

I waited calmly, happy to be in his well-appointed courtyard again so soon. Beautiful late morning sunshine pulsed down from blue skies, making the orange roses adorning his castle show off their hues with extra emphasis. Helmut lay off to the side ten yards away or so from us, watching, but without concern. It appeared I'd now become a second thought to the dog, after the Culp and Clifton skirmish. I had a hunch Helmut wanted another piece of Culp, probably envisioning that slug secured in his jaws for a good shaking. I'd be glad to pull up a chair with some popcorn for such an event. Would it happen again? Unlikely. But hope springs eternal.

Ah, foodstuffs. Already on the table in front of me, sealed up nice and tight in plastic wrap, sat a heavy bundle of noodles. About twice what we normally receive as payment. One look at the booty, I knew nagging hunger would be a thing of the past, at least until that bundle ran out. We were talking two full weeks of eating for three people, if the portions were sensible. I particularly hate sensible portions, but you have to sacrifice when necessary. Add in two or three harvested rabbits, a bucket of fish all filleted up, a discovered larder of canned goods in some abandoned basement, or if divine good fortune smiled down upon us, a butchered adult deer, we were set for twice that long. Oh, the possibilities.

Graves then set down a small bag of pine nuts, next to the noodle gold mine. These little nuts, mostly from white pines in the region, are a product the Minnow Man ventures a fair distance to collect. Pine nuts are tasty, nutritious, and hard to come across in this area. They're thus perfect as a gift, especially as a way to show someone your appreciation. And to solidify their loyalty. If Graves knew anything, it was the art of the deal.

"Regarding your question: of course I know the location," Graves said. "I described the resource to Culp and Clifton in the first place. The location of the product was the Minnow Man's discovery. Nothing surprising there."

"Well, why not just have the Minnow Man collect the product for you?" I said.

"Culp and Clifton would execute Horace, our Minnow Man, in short order," Graves said.

"But the Minnow Man is a master of stealth. He'd out-maneuver them."

"How many times? Once? Twice? A third time? Until their bullets connected. Remember, our Minnow Man is a non-combatant."

"Why me and my ladies then? Are we expendable?" I said.

"No, you're combatants. Especially you," Graves said.

"I don't want any more trouble than I already have," I said. "I'll skip the combat if possible."

"Please, Trick Chasseur. Don't yank my chain. You'd take the opportunity to engage in combat any time you could. If the situation was right. The odds in your favor and all."

"Uh, Mortimer, what do you make me out to be?"

Graves paused for a moment, looking me over. Enjoying it as I squirmed. His eyes still had a little of that glow from last night. The bright sun reduced the glow's intensity, however. Camouflaged it. Which was convenient, not seeing the glow in its full strangeness. And I instinctively knew the glow shouldn't be there. Not that obviously, anyway. Not if trouble with the boss man himself was to be avoided.

"Answer me honestly. You have in your hand a full bucket of harvested crops," Graves said. "You are attacked…unprovoked, and they mean to kill you. You, as it happens, kill them instead. What seems better to you? The life-giving haul of the crops in your possession? Or you, standing triumphant over the ones who tried to kill you? With your gun, knife, or even the solid toes of your kicking boots on your feet…and watching the last breaths of life leak from your assailants?"

I said nothing.

"Conquered opponents, enemies who deserve to die, versus your food. Which gives you a more significant burst of satisfaction, deep down in your lizard brain?"

I still said nothing. I knew the answer, and so did Mortimer Graves. Maybe something was wrong with me. I reveled in the conquest, the victory. In brutality. Maybe I was a bad guy too. But there was no one around to determine if that was the case or not. I myself couldn't. Margo and Ruby were first and foremost trying to survive, not referee the psychological development in their guy. And Graves…he wouldn't pass judgment on my tendencies. In fact, I'm pretty sure he liked that aspect of me.

"Opponents who deserve to die, like Culp and Clifton. It's looking like they had something up their sleeve for you and your partners, my friend," Graves said. "Something bad. I never would have set up the cooperative effort with them if I'd known."

If I'd known. Once again, I didn't respond, because I, conversely, had known. And should have known better than to go through with the project. Forget about what Graves had a sense of or not. So sophisticated, so high and mighty. He had a fraction of what I did in real-life combat, maybe less than that. Secure in his ivory tower, with his high voltage fence and gate, his security cameras taking in everything. His grizzly bear of a dog. Maybe Graves really, sincerely, had not known those two creeps planned a double-cross. He bought their bullshit and put my partners and me in serious danger. Damn. Never again. I'd never in the future walk into something like that acorn harvest with guys such as those two. And even more so, never again put my ladies at risk in such a way. Even if it meant going hungry. Skinny is better than dead.

Matter of fact, I shouldn't have let those two bastards walk away. Once I sensed what was going on, with their nefarious plans in the works for my trio, I should have iced them. The possibility of their evil intentions now looked more and more definite, as the two men had arrived with guns but no plans to actually work. Clifton trying to take control of my project the moment they showed up. Attempting to separate the women and me.

Shouldn't have let them get away. I pondered that very thought as I sat with Graves that morning, not knowing that it was the most important truism I'd never acted upon. Didn't know how significant it was then, but I would soon.

"So, as I mentioned, you'll be collecting lichen off certain trees back in the wetland. Lichen is common on trees and rocks, in places where the air is healthy. Like this area."

I nodded. We'd already went through this info, just twenty minutes ago. Graves had pronounced it "lye-ken." Never heard of it before that moment. But of course, I hadn't heard of quite a few things.

"Not all of the lichen is the correct stuff. I'll arrange for the Minnow Man to meet you back in the swamp, and he'll describe to you the difference."

My mind was wandering to the new task we'd been hired for, considering payoffs, profit, feasibility, and risk. Especially risk; risk, as in ambush by rifle.

"I need the lichen for my medicine," Graves continued. "I figured Culp and Clifton would be willing to seek it out and bring it back, in return for plenty of food and medicine. It went well until recently."

I nodded, remained quiet, and continued to listen. Graves most likely knew my mind was on the new project, and on the extra food we were now receiving, and on Culp and Clifton. He understood such things, the silent calculations and ponderings of a thinker, that person keeping most of their thoughts to themselves. Besides, he was always glad to have the floor, for a chance to talk and talk. He continued.

"Your group should be able to make a bigger haul in less time than those two idiots," Graves said. "The Minnow Man has had them under surveillance. Watched them several times. To say they pegged production would be an understatement. They worked casually, resting a lot, gabbing. Yet they'd speak of incredible efforts to get the lichen. Not sure if I was paying them enough for such backbreaking work."

I shook my head, agreeing with his take on it. "We'll do better. We're faster. Cheaper. Better looking," I said. "Why weren't we brought in on this lichen collection stuff sooner?"

"I refrained from informing you, Master Trick, as you had other tasks just as important to me."

"Cutting your grass?"

"Don't belittle what you do. Having these grounds kept pristine lifts my spirits. Reminds me of the splendid old days. Keeps me positive. Keeps me...medicating."

I understood. Lest he go zombie positive.

"Besides...you think that big ruffian can live on dandelion leaves and acorns?" Graves said, nodding at Helmut. "We absolutely need those minnows and small fish. That's the Minnow Man's niche. Yours is the lawn care coupled with gathering maple and oak products. Freeing Horace up for his minnow catching specialty. Which is why Culp and Clifton getting involved in the lichen collection worked so well."

"Until it didn't," I said.

"Precisely."

I glanced over to Helmut, who kept a lazy watch on our meeting. Looking bored. Good.

"Besides, I didn't want to have you offsite any more than needed. You offer protection with your presence," Graves said.

"Me? How about your own aura? I'd bet you've made more than one person think twice about pulling something over on you," I said. "With, you know, your image and all."

"That's smart on their part, in my estimation. But I consider you a person amongst my inner circle. You'd have my back. You're like family to me. And that's rare. For example, people such as your lady friends are not. They are your subcontractors. I value them too. But I don't see why they'd risk their safety to help me."

"Back up. They're my lovers. My loved ones, not just—"

"They're not originally from here, you are."

"What difference–"

"That's how inner circles stay inner. But regardless," Graves continued. I didn't interrupt. Hey, he's the boss. "If no meds, then I turn. Transition. Then it's over. I actually want to do it sometimes. Like when those sons of bitches Culp and Clifton confronted me. So easy to give in to the lust of transforming. Tempting. But I can't let myself. Not ever."

I waited. I looked at the mansion. At the greenery in the area. At the roses. Even at Helmut, seeing if he could bail me out of this conversation…just to illustrate how uncomfortable it was getting.

"In any event, you need to make that harvest for me. Really need to. I've been running dangerously low on the medicine, my friend. You haven't seemed to notice any differences, I think. Your friends, the ladies, are sometimes more alert than you, Trick."

That got my attention.

"Meaning?" I said.

"That I've been dangerously close lately. I can tell that they recognize it, the both of them. They see something in my demeanor, my gaze…"

Like glowing, haunted, craven eyes? All three of us saw it. I was simply doing stealth diplomacy by pretending not to notice. I wanted to say all that, but let it go instead.

"I think they know if I transformed I'd try to kill and eat them. So they're exhibiting appropriate apprehension, as far as I'm concerned. I can see how they look back at me."

He'd been paying attention to the green field as he said it, his expression one a state of sadness, possibly of regret. Graves looked back to my eyes then, a hint of that gaze he guessed Ruby and Margo feared. A hungry gaze.

"And if I had the chance, my friend, while in the zombie state, I'd kill and eat you along with them."

"Or die trying," I said.

That one blurted out of me, but it wasn't untrue. It was the real Trick Chasseur, but I maybe should have withheld the comment regardless.

Graves stayed fixed on my eyes with a steady look, then a ghost of that enchanting yet terrifying smile formed on his arrogant face.

"There's my boy," he said.

Maybe no need to hold back on it after all. I guess my attitude was part of why he kept me around.

"I'm not infallible or immortal. I need protection, or I can't ever venture from the mansion. One bullet to the head would make me cease to exist, just like anyone else."

"If the attack was done from afar," I said.

"Exactly."

"And up close?"

"Hand to hand?"

"Yeah."

"We'd have to see. Despite my age, my strength... has seemed to increase."

He again looked off into the distance, to the Hemlock and Tamarack swamp, to the lush green field in front of it. This time he looked pleased, however, not distressed.

"Because, well..."

"Again, the initial stages of transition. I know," I said. Like any of the zombie horde, he had paradoxically gained strength while swimming in the reality of living death. He'd told me last year that he was keeping himself in tip-top condition inside the mansion, starting back up with a routine he'd done in his college swordplay heyday. Gymnastics. On parallel bars and rings. And the old boy was, what, 80 or so?

"Yes, since then," Graves said. "The new vigor ramping up due to the combination of the medication and the new muscle cells related to the transition, I suppose. But regarding the showdown you propose, with a commando, like some of the surviving ex-military drifters that occasionally come through, well…they'd probably be able to handle me in a tussle. That's my guess."

"How about if each of you had a primitive weapon? Say, for instance, a sword?"

There was that partial smile again. Spooky like always, but in this case I knew where Mortimer Graves was going with it. And I liked it. The good guys against the bad guys. Or at least my team against the other team. I smiled back.

"A sword. Surely you jest," Graves said.

"Surely I don't. Each of you have a sword. But the other guy's formidable. A soldier, or like you stated, a commando. At least an enthusiast of fighting."

"But not a champion fencer or trained sword wielder?"

"No. Just a brute with a blade, ready for some swashbuckling."

"Then I'd carve him up like a tube of pepperoni."

I stood then, picking up the noodles and pine nuts. Before leaving I nodded to Mortimer Graves, trying the best I could to mirror that hint of a smile he'd given me.

"There's my man," I said.

13

Wine. Dandelion wine. Sweet, sweet dandelion wine. I took another sip. Ah. Perfect. And within that same night, things were about to get a lot sweeter for your narrator. A lot hotter. It helps to have the virility I do. And the magnetism. And a boss that distributes wine to his employees…including a bottle to each of my delightful lovers.

Sweet, sweet wine. Thank you, Mortimer Graves.

Background: a celebration was underway. The harvest was in. Not much trouble in delivering it. Surprisingly easy, actually. And the payoff was *outstanding*.

One small jar of crabapple jelly. A dozen protein pucks, which are a combo of rabbit and fish fillets, with about five types of seeds ground up and mixed in. Some kind of tasty spice addition too. High in protein, thus life-sustaining. Delicious as well. They'd help hold us over on our pilgrimage to Texas.

As a final kind gesture in the trading, Graves handed off to each of us a bottle of dandelion wine. In the spring, dandelions make a bright yellow carpet in the surrounding fields; popping off the yellow gems and bringing them in is simple. We harvest some for the lord of the manor, as does the Minnow Man. Graves picks a bunch himself, namely the dandelions which settle themselves in a poorly chosen growth plan: inside his fenced enclosure. Old Man Graves sees each dandelion as product. The leaves and roots as salad ingredients, the flowers as another future swirl of dandelion wine. Pop goes the dandelion. End of story. Until the salad is served and the wine is ready.

The resulting dandelion wine is strong in flavor and white in color. Each year, Graves produces about 20 bottles of the stuff. He consumes about 15 or 16 of those himself. The rest are saved for gifts, like we'd received. The dandelion wine starts out in some kind of vat in his basement, and once done, it's distributed to smaller glass containers, capped, then the top sealed with plastic. For simplicity, Graves uses old Snapple bottles, Snapple having once been a popular commercial drink. The company claimed it was made from the best stuff on earth, and it may have been, then. But nowadays I think Graves' wine would trump it in a taste test. In any case, unlike *le vin de Graves,* Snapple would not get a person drunk.

Which we were just then.

It was the wine's fault. And that wine had been earned so easily, no less. The major lichen collection project, basically scraping and peeling the delicate lichen off of swampland trees, was a cinch. Compared to an acorn harvest, the collection of lichen was but a warmup. This was the claim to fame of Culp and Clifton? No wonder they stayed at the level they were at.

And the top secret knowledge a person needed to successfully select the correct lichen? To get just the right type, so it was the perfect contribution to the anti-zombie antidote? It took the Minnow Man about seven seconds to explain it.

The wavy little sections of lichen which grew on the Hemlock trees was the right stuff. The lichen which grew on the similar Tamarack trees was the wrong stuff. Something about what was in the sap of the Hemlock trees made that lichen perfect. That lichen on the Tamarack tree trunks, in contrast, wouldn't work. Pick the Hemlock type, leave the Tamarack type. Mind-boggling details. We went to work.

Hours later, we delivered a three-gallon bucket full of the lichen to the mansion. Graves looked like a drowning swimmer just thrown a lifesaver. We followed our simplistic but heroic shuttling of lichen material from swamp to mansion with the devouring of a hefty takeout container of noodles that the boss had sent us away with. They'd been cooked up, buttered, and mixed with herbs and cherry tomatoes, and went down eagerly and easily into hungry stomachs. Satiated and becoming sleepy, we luxuriated in the barn. Sipping, savoring.

I was on my bed, minding my own business, looking with sadness into my little wine bottle. There was but an ounce or so left. Just an ounce. Sad. Almost tragic.

The sadness wasn't to last. My babes made their move.

Margo slid onto the bed next to me, only underwear and a sleeveless tee thing on all of a sudden. We'd all been in fieldwork togs but a minute ago. So far this was not a shock. The interlude was due for the two of us. But later in the night, once Ruby was asleep, ideally.

It made some thoughts jump into my mind. What about our other partner? A little soon, isn't it? The correct order of the rotation. Aren't we going…I felt the weight on the bed of a third person. The both of them? What?

Then Ruby started in. Lower. My jeans being undone. Uh-oh.

"I have rules…" I started. Margo's mouth covered mine. I shut up for a few seconds. That was… insubordination. I let it go for a few seconds, though. Then a few more. I came up for air, when she went lower for an earlobe nibble thing. It tripped up my complaint. I could barely function as a dictator.

"This isn't…we have principles to follow. We can't veer off course like this," I said. "We…"

Now it was Ruby, also insubordinate, her delicate fingertips running along my cheek, and then onto my lips. Hushing me. Hey! Were they on to some new kick of making me shut up?

"Yes we can," Ruby said. "Just watch us."

Mutiny! I couldn't get myself to fight it off, not just yet. Traitors!

More of the nibble thing. The other one with the fingertip thing. My resolve to make it cease was failing to build. I protested, silently.

"Something you've never done, Trick, but there's no time like the present to learn. Don't worry about it. Just let it happen," Margo said, as Ruby giggled.

That was it! They were on to me! The little factoids, cowering in the back of my mind. Embarrassment. Inexperience. Uncertainty. Loss of control. Ineptitude. What if all of that came to the forefront? What if several years of building up an image suddenly vanished? In one moment of ménage madness?

But…loss of control was upon me. The slippery slope might as well have been coated in massage oil. I gave in.

Again, it was the wine's fault.

Lucky for us all, I'm a fast learner.

14

We woke just after dawn. Got all washed up with hot, soapy water, then feasted on a breakfast of tasty noodles and pine nuts. Rested and ready. Just had to make our last trade of the year with Mortimer Graves, jump onto our prepped cycles and then float down the freeway, heading south.

I remember that morning, autumn in the North starting to ramp up in its grandeur. The crisp feeling and collection of smells that only a cold night and frosty morning can impart on a world of luscious green grass and colorful leaves. Especially once the morning sun comes out to bake them. At the time, I believed that I couldn't have felt any more wonderful. That I couldn't have been enveloped in a better sense of well being.

And I thought it would be a tremendous day. If I had only known.

***

First thing we did was head straight to the edge of the field, where it changes into swampland. A small patch of wild strawberries flourished there, with berries that were at that almost ripe stage. We'd picked them as a small show of appreciation to Mortimer Graves. Even if the berries weren't quite ripe, Graves can use them. Mainly he purees them into either his jam, which also includes the portions of crabapple, raspberry, and some wildflower petals, or his vinaigrette salad dressing. The extra tartness adds to its value as a salad enhancement, he's claimed. Sure, I guess it does, but I for one am not that picky. If it's good for you, just put it on the leaves and eat it, I say. Anyway, those berries were to be a goodwill gesture toward Mortimer Graves. On the house, you could say.

We got whatever berries we could find picked and bagged, a handful of them I think, and we began our short trudge over to the mansion. Past the barn, where our cycles waited, toward the mansion. The two ladies hustled along just ahead of me, both with a firearm in the crook of an arm, looking boisterous and jubilant. Victory in the air, regarding yesterday's harvest of the product for Graves, crucial for his antidote. Happy about the harvest and all the resulting food and extra fuel that went along with it. And a tiny pinch of extra medicine had been earned by our efforts, the valuable penicillin-plus stuff Graves manufactured. We were going to make out like bandits, and we were heading down to Texas, to continued sunshine. Well before this place turned into one giant freezer. Joy in our hearts, and for good reason.

**

Margo was ahead of me just then, and Ruby immediately behind. Ruby wrapped her arm around my neck. Her hot breath was traveling into my ear, the soft body pressing against me, and looking her way I saw once again the smooth neck underneath her round face, dark eyes anchoring the center of her countenance. Saying quietly she had special plans for me once we got down south, what exactly I now can't remember. Talking quietly. She didn't have to do such flirtations on the sly, but she had class enough to be discreet when possible. And if Margo noticed and got jealous? She wouldn't; she rarely got jealous. Margo was normally too self-contained to let herself appear flustered. Plus, she cared about

Ruby, and wanted to see her happy. As a matter of fact, I'd just found out Margo had even helped Ruby achieve said happiness at times. Specifically, as demonstrated in that three-person thing that they'd just introduced me to last night. I still didn't think it was a good idea. But I'll admit, while the three-at-once deal seemed wrong, it sure felt right. Do it again? I was leaning toward a yes. Although at that moment, I still was feeling a little worn out. I figured I'd see what happened as things progressed.

I also remember thinking at the time: it's good to be alive. And so good to be accompanied by loving women.

Then I stopped thinking about anything on that subject. Completely. We stopped walking, and took in the scene just ahead.

The gate to the grounds was wide open. I'd never witnessed that before. The mansion door was agape. Never had seen that either. The place was unguarded and silent. No Graves to be found anywhere.

Something was wrong. Even at that point it seemed so. But we hadn't seen anything yet. We stepped into the courtyard. I told the women to wait back a ways, and I stepped forward, closer to the open front door.

A big shadowy bulk materialized in the dim light of the foyer. It came closer. A face full of fury, sporting jaws that could crush the bones of a human femur. A face full of menace. Eyes focused, clearly agitated, powerful legs quaking in anticipation. The oversized watchdog from hell.

Helmut the Bull Mastiff. Staring straight at us. And now with no master to call it back.

Ah, fuck.

Not knowing the full situation here, I didn't want to unleash the double barrel blasts on the fearsome canine in front of me. Not yet. I set my shotgun down on one of Graves' little decorative garden walls. A major mistake as it turned out, parting with my gun. I then unstrapped the pole pruner from my back. I uncovered the machete blade, and extended the telescoping pole. Hoping that if the dog's unfriendly looks ramped up – as in it charging us – I could simply ward it off for a moment or two. In case Graves appeared and took control.

I didn't get it yet. I soon would.

The dog stepped forward. Not with aggression. Not with confidence. Rather, with trepidation, with fear… and with a whine, it looked up at me. Seeking help.

That's when I knew things were seriously hosed.

My first thoughts upon seeing the big dog staring out at us: had Helmut done something to Graves? Had this monster of a dog turned on its master?

I had it exactly the opposite.

15

Helmut was looking askance at me for help. 700-pound Helmut! Or whatever the chunky thing weighed. Bigger than me, I know that much. Yes, things already felt weird, but after Helmut showed his sheepishness, I suddenly sensed something more forbidding was on its way. That things were going to graduate from simply weird to bad…and I was right.

That's when the bullets began to fly.

***

The first sign of attack was a sharp crack of a single rifle shot. Then two more shots popped through the air, and two corresponding little powder bursts erupted on the mansion's stone exterior near me. I stumbled backward, hearing more shots piercing the air, my eyes seeking the ladies, spotting Margo, seeing her with the shotgun up, blasting shots, two, three, four…no, empty after three it looked like. I saw her turn to run, straight from the mansion, to the dense weeds. Ruby was nowhere to be seen. About to sprint to my shotgun, which I'd mistakenly set down, but the disgusting Kevin Culp blocked my path to it. With a rifle. Pointed my way. A bullet smacked a patio chair right next to me – and I turned to run inside the mansion, my mind racing, looking for options, another bullet shattering a light fixture above me. Once inside, I turned to see that sonofabitch Culp lunging through the mansion's front door, raising his .22 rifle, readying another shot.

***

I had turned to run, to scramble, into a dwelling I'd never before set foot in. No gun now, just my pole pruner. After yet another bullet whizzed past my head, I got down near the floor, and started to rush left then right, making my course a purposely erratic path. Harder to hit. I dropped the pole pruner, turned to scoop it up, and when another bullet burst the tile on the floor next to it, I rushed ahead without it.

I could hear Culp's slamming footsteps from behind. One heavy footfall followed by a drag, over and over, as he favored the leg Helmut had sunk long teeth into a short time ago. And Helmut was scrambling like mad, not turning to attack Culp, but running and thrashing along by my side. Something had really thrown the bulky watchdog off his game. Following me for protection, in a blind panic. Insanity. No time to think about it. Down a long, dimly lit, ornate hall, the dog and I continued rushing like panicked rodents. Another .22 slug popped our way, center punching a colorful vase set on a ledge along the wall. Probably an antique worth 20 grand or more in the past. No hallway or door to turn off into, not yet. Culp's voice, angry and amused, came booming down the corridor.

"We got one of ya down!"

One down?

"And looks like yer next, ya skinny little prick!" Culp said.

I saw a possible piece of protection: a big, decorative shield on the wall, next to some kind of aged suit of armor. Helmut stopped near me, rattled, panicked, saw the lowlife Culp closing in, started running away, then came back in confusion, drawing a shot from Culp's rifle.

Pop!

Then the squeal of a ricochet. Another miss, the dog difficult to sight in as it darted frantically. I yanked the shield from the wall, pulling out some wall hooks in the process, powder from ancient plaster coming out with it. Shield whipped up quick, to guard as much of myself as possible, barely looking over the top of it, backing up. Culp turned the .22 rifle in my direction.

Pop! Ping!

The shield was real, not a prop, and so far bullet proof. I backed up more, looking over my shoulder for an instant down the hall, finally seeing a big, wide door on the left side of the hallway. Where it went, who could know.

Culp repositioned himself, looking past me at Helmut, then to me. Who to shoot at next, with the gun's limited ammo. I was closer, Helmut was Helmut, and potentially dangerous. Not dangerous right now, though. Then a loud boom sounded from behind Culp, coming down the hall we'd just scrambled through, the explosive sound traveling to us from the open door of the mansion. Clearly a gunshot. From the courtyard and field outside. Where the women were. And almost certainly the scumbag Kevin Clifton.

A crooked expression creased Culp's horrid face, a look that he probably thought was a smile.

"And now I believe we got two of ya down. Heh."

I continued holding the heavy shield. Two down? Following the blast of a gun. Could only mean one thing. If he was right…I considered throwing the massive shield at Culp, then trying to lunge past him and hope he missed with any shots, if the shield didn't in fact connect. Or rush him, the shield in front…if a scuffle resulted, maybe get in a hard kick to his head or midsection, deflate him…then grab his rifle.

"Oh, yeah!" bellowed Amos Culp. Happy. "Screw us

out of what's ours, will ya? Well, we're here to claim it. And a whole lot more. You're going down next, with the old bastard's dog. Then Graves himself is going down. We're taking the whole place over!"

Throw the shield, or run forward with it, or drop it and run straight away down the long dark hall. Had to do something. What, what?!

Then – with the speed of a lightning bolt, a change came upon the situation.

A dog's yelp from behind me; a whoosh of footsteps from the same direction; Culp stopped looking at me, instead switching attention further down the hallway. Helmut sprinted past me and then past Culp, Culp ignoring the dog. His amusement now gone, a look of intense alarm replacing it and lighting up his homely face.

Another series of thudding footsteps, from behind me, soon close, almost touching me…I whirled!

Raising the shield just in time, I blocked the chopping motion of a huge, shiny blade.

Clang!

I was nearly knocked off my feet, regained my footing, and intercepted another flash of steel, coming from above, aimed right at the top of my head.

Clang!

The blade was like a meat cleaver Godzilla would wield.

I saw the new assailant as I was backing up, right toward Culp – yes, toward Culp!

Yep, saw the new assailant.

Mortimer Graves.

Only not the Mortimer Graves we've come to know. Same natty suit, bowtie neatly in place. Today's tie was blood red. How fitting. Planning ahead? His eyes now glowing with a silvery light, pupils barely visible, facial skin drooping. As if it was not long from falling off the bone. Dark veins now pronounced under pale skin.

Swoosh! Clang!

Another sword swipe, impact even harder now as Graves – or the partial Graves – got into the groove. Warmed up now, in the zone for ruthless murder.

Swoosh! Clang!

Another swing and a miss, at least missing my body, the shield blessedly holding out.

A blast sounded from Culp's gun, aimed at Graves but with no effect, and the sword came down again, colliding with the wide shield and making it gong like a church bell, sending me backpedaling. The shield hit the floor along with me. I scrambled away from the both of them. Toward my machete on a stick.

I picked up the pole pruner, and turned back toward Graves' location, ready to swing it in defense.

But Graves was otherwise engaged for the moment. Culp had the rifle up, popped off a shot at Graves' midsection, then jumped back to avoid a sword swing.

Have fun folks.

I turned to run, to escape the mansion completely. I could hear some motorized apparatus up ahead working. I took a microsecond to glance back.

The old freak Graves, methodical despite his transitioning, had moved back away from Culp and removed his remote from his suit pocket. Pointed it and clicked it. In one of the most terrifying moments of my life, I heard it.

The mansion's door closing, sealing itself shut with authority. With finality.

***

It wasn't time to stop my momentum, sealed

mansion door or not. I fled around the corner and straight to the huge door. I'd find a way to open it and get out for good…only I couldn't. The door had one hefty, sturdy handle on it, and it didn't budge. Nothing else to grab. A shoulder pressed into it with full power resulted in no progress; it was like trying to move a bridge piling.

Damn you and your fancy remote controls, Graves.

I'd been in countless jams before. This would just be one more, although admittedly weirder than any other. Two monstrosities confronted each other down the hallway: one wanted to shoot me, the other wanted to slice me in two with a massive, historic sword. No problem…kind of. My usual response for such situations had to be followed: outthink, outdo, or outmaneuver the opponents. Then fuck 'em up so bad they can't recover …or just kill them. I wasn't bloodthirsty, still am not, but I believe in waking up the next morning to greet a new day. Can't do that with a bullet through your brain, or your body all chopped up.

I proceeded, pole pruner tipped with its machete in my hands, stepping their way slowly now, Helmut sticking close behind me. The main key here: Culp's rifle had to run empty. It had to, Graves still fighting or not, because I had no shield anymore. Only place to run was through that mysterious door down the hall, past the two figures now facing off against each other. If Culp executed Graves, and I ran past, he could just shoot me in the back.

I wouldn't need to get past them, though…because I was going to take both opponents out with my machete blade. Now. I'd decided to, at least. Easier said than done.

I continued viewing their confrontation: Culp shot another slug at Graves, aiming for his chest as Graves tried a sword swing, the bullet seemed to miss, and Culp pointed the gun at Graves' head next.

Click.

Finally out of ammo. Poor Culp.

He backed up away from Graves, who readied the sword once again, and Culp did the sensible thing, to my surprise. He turned the gun around, gripping the barrel like a club. Better than nothing. Graves made a low slash then, and Culp smacked it away with the wooden gun butt club. One for one, Culp, I thought. Can you keep it up?

Wouldn't matter. I had to get outside, to defend or save Ruby and Margo. These two weirdos were to be taken care of, now. I'd end the threat, machete style.

Graves caught Culp with a shallow stab in the gut; Culp collapsed backwards. While still on the floor, Culp started quickly reaching for his fallen gun, his makeshift club, his only hope.

There was my chance, right then. I surged up, in an instant stopping just a few feet from Graves. He turned from his victim on the floor, who appeared to be down for good, to his next one, me, standing near him with a long, simplistic weapon.

Graves assumed some kind of sword fighter's stance; I think that's what it was. Didn't matter: he had a three-foot sword, I had a nine-foot pole pruner, adorned with a two-foot long brush-chopping machete on its end. He was toast.

Figured I'd give him an impromptu last rites statement. He had been a good boss, after all. I couldn't just execute him. Lots of history between us. He'd supplied me with so much. But one look at him now, and it was clear all that was over. He wasn't the same person any more. Not a person at all, really.

Plus, I thought a lofty verbal announcement might

confuse him, make him pause…so I could strike him dead with ease.

"Mr. Mortimer Graves, Lord of the Manor…" I began.

His silvery, brilliant eyes with no visible pupils looked back at me. No sign of being impressed.

"You have indicated with your actions that those humans in your proximity are to be slain by sword. Probably followed by you eating them. I oppose this gesture, and overrule it," I said.

I was trying to sound pompous like Graves himself, to give him an appropriate sendoff. I've read a lot of books in the past few years, remember? It's all I could think of. But let's face it, this old coot had no chance considering what faced him now. I felt kind of bad for Graves. This was the end. Even the swordsman's stance he'd assumed looked lame. Graves was hunched forward, the sword hanging down, its tip almost touching the floor.

"And the Duke of the Wetlands and Forest – Trick Chasseur – decrees you shall cease to be a threat. You… er…thou, are formally sentenced to death by beheading."

Don't delay, I figured. Don't make the old man suffer more than needed. It's over – now!

I swung.

Apparently it wasn't over, I decided, when ¾ of my machete blade clinked to the stone floor, severed from the rest of the tool. One slice of his huge sword, straight through the blade of my machete. Whoa.

My machete used to retail for around $16, his sword was probably worth thousands. Guess you get what you pay for.

I jumped back, landing on the floor, avoiding Graves' next razor sharp swish, that one a backhand. I was up in an instant, ready for his following attacks.

Wondering how the piece of blade, just inches long now, atop a skinny pole made of fiberglass tubing material, would withstand direct sword blows. Answer: it wouldn't.

"You hurt me, freak, now I'm gonna bust you up!" Culp yelled from behind Graves. Graves whirled from me to Culp. The dork Culp had made it back to his feet; he was bleeding from his belly, but was not giving up. Ready to take another swing at Graves, he of the shaving-sharp medieval sword.

A distraction! Culp, you finally did something right. I took the chance and hustled down the hall, deeper into the mansion, toward the mystery door on the side of the hallway. My only hope, it seemed. Perhaps a stairway to the upper floors, maybe a back exit. A tunnel? A pit? I'd have taken any of them right then. I grabbed the handle, twisted; it was in fact unlocked. Yes! I opened it, ready to step in, Helmut behind me, ready to follow.

Oh. A janitorial closet. Mops, buckets, brooms, rags. I stepped in anyway, letting the dog follow. I closed the door most of the way, leaving a half-inch crack from which to watch. In a way I wish I hadn't done that.

Culp was being eviscerated, then chopped, then chopped further. Man oh man. Guess that's what a big battle sword does best. Couldn't happen to a nicer piece of garbage than Culp, either. Still not easy to watch, though.

Did the same fate await me? Then the dog? Do something, Trick. Think! Take his knees out with the pole? Throw it like a spear? Then, I remembered…

I felt into my hip pack, which I always have on when we ride. Moved my hand a moment, feeling…there it was. The case housing the antidote needle. Safe and secure, and loaded with a single, potent dose of the stuff. Filled with the same compound Graves needed to stay human. The medicine that it looked like Graves had somehow ran short of. Or decided to not take.

Worth a try; at least if I ended up in pieces, I'd have given it a go. The machete had a dial-on attachment I'd rigged up, with supporting clamps. The hypodermic could fit in that same spot, and while there was no threading of any kind, the clamps would secure it without question. No more difficult than dialing a water faucet off.

Despite having only a slight sliver of light to work by, I proceeded. Done in 21 seconds. I smacked Helmut on the snout when he started to whine in terror. He stopped. I peeked back out. There was a zombie man standing, and a diabolical former man – now a corpse – sprawled out with indescribable wounds, and plenty of spreading blood. Little else.

The blood apparently had Mortimer Graves mesmerized. He stared down at it. For a bit. Then he looked up. And back down the hall. Straight at the closet the dog and I cowered in.

Sword held down low, relaxed and ready, he started walking. Heading directly for us.

16

I opened the closet door, let it swing open, and lowered the pole with the hypodermic needle affixed to its end. Ready to stab, to inject. It would be good for one thrust only.

Graves held the sword in front of him, an illustrious light fixture overhead causing a yellow gleam to ricochet off its length. The blade's edge was meant for me, for my demise. To prepare my body for being eaten. It balanced there, about to fly into action…the shiny sword he'd just used to slice apart Culp.

I realized that I knew that sword. He'd been so proud to display it to me last summer; the sword's lines, its grip. The sword's razor-like edge. It was Graves' favorite. And of course, he'd named it.

Attila. Named after the insatiable murderer Attila the Hun, of course. Splendid.

And what a person to give such a blade to. Graves had not been trained in simplistic swordplay. He hadn't explored it at an introductory level, like someone taking Strip Mall Martial Arts 101. Graves had competed in it, at that McGill place up in Montpelier or Montreal or somewhere. And this particular showdown offered worse odds for yours truly than just those factors. It wouldn't be just a fight against a fencer. Normally a fencer uses a competition sword, like a pointy foil or the slender edged saber. But those are lightweight tools. Not some oversized dinosaur fang made of steel, like Graves was holding now.

Let me help you envision this sword. Imagine a straight razor, like fancy barber shops used to have. But make that razor about three feet long, and weighing, oh, I don't know, 80 pounds? Or 90? Plus, it had a point on it that looked as sharp as an ice pick. Getting the picture?

And I'd been worried about that mongrel Helmut? As in the same dog now crouched behind me, hiding.

But hiding or not…the dog and I had to face the music. Face Mortimer Graves…no longer seeming like a Zombie Billionaire, but rather a Zombie Berserker.

The dog and I remained in the janitorial closet. The old tycoon, now transitioned into demon form, made his first step forward…tentatively. His eyes on mine, then on my center mass, watching for motion. Ready to counter me if I made a move. Eyes flickering over to that bulldozer with fangs, Helmut, then back to me. Figuring that maybe Young Trick in front of him was a bit more formidable, more crafty, than the last adversary he'd faced. That adversary being the dipshit Culp, who now sprawled with multiple slices on his body, literally butchered, on the floor of the mansion.

Graves was anticipating that I'd be more crafty. He had that right. For Young Trick had yet another trick up his sleeve. It involved substantial risk. Caution thrown to the wind. Fearlessness. Daring. Danger.

But, hey, it wasn't my dog.

I placed my boot on the butt of the big growling machine known as Helmut, the Bull Mastiff with the prick attitude; yeah, the overgrown dog who was now whining like a petrified little kid. Face it, if I didn't send the dog forward, we would have both been carved up with Graves' sword. Or at least Helmut would have been, while I scrambled past the action to try the front door again. But I planned to save the dog. And myself. And even Graves, no less.

"Time to show your stuff, you big bastard. Go!" I yelled at the dog, thrusting my foot against his flank, the dog then tumbling toward its master.

Graves took the bait. His focus turned from me to his pet, to his constant companion. And his next blood feast, if he could manage it. He whirled, sword in hand, following the motion of the panicked Helmut, as the dog gained purchase on the tiles underfoot and scrambled to get away. To escape his owner Mortimer Graves, and that master's other pet, the sword named Attila.

For such a locomotive-sized dog, the canine did move with some agility; grace under terror, you could say. Graves swung the heavy steel near the flailing dog's side, missing, then into the air again, fruitlessly, as Helmut ran in a semi-circle toward the front of door of the mansion. Graves turned in that direction, his right side now to me. The front door of course was closed, with no one to open it for the dog. So Helmut did an about face, and ran back in the same direction it had come from. Putting Graves in the middle of me and the path on which the dog ran. Graves readjusted, ready to intercept Helmut for the kill. In order to do so, Graves had to turn his back to me. Good dog.

He raised the sword, ready to chop it down onto the confused and frantic Helmut. Then Graves let the sword drop, his face now aimed at the arched ceiling of the mansion, and soon bursting out into a shrill scream.

I'd just thrust the end of the pole pruner, with the filled hypodermic needle, into the left side of Graves' zombie rump. And I drove him forward, right into the rock wall of his hallway. He screamed again...no, make that a roar. God, like nothing I'd ever heard before. He tried to whirl, to free himself from the needle puncturing him, then tried to turn the other way. He could do neither, as I kept the pressure on. And on. Full Trick Chasseur now, putting all my weight, and arm, shoulder and leg strength into it. I hadn't developed these muscles for nothing, with all those martial arts workouts, all those long swims, hilly hikes, and lengthy dumbbell sessions. And all those drag-outs of dead deer from swamps and forests, deer the same size as me. Fights with the street brawlers and football guys long ago in the alley near my high school, protecting my weaker friends. My muscles weren't for show. Well, back in the days of the normal world they kind of were, but now they were made to deliver. That was a very good thing to possess right then.

At first it was difficult to pin Graves there. A squeal, another roar, a yell…all causing plenty of volume to echo in the mansion's dark, magnificent hall and adjoining atrium. A head swing, trying to look at me with a full snarl, a futile reach behind him with each arm for the pole, a few slams on the wall with closed fists in frustration as I kept the raging character anchored there.

Then his tenacity, his ferocity, started to dissipate. The twisting and flailing of his arms and torso ceased, a sort of a calm taking over. Or maybe it was just the wilting that comes with defeat. And it appeared to be influenced by exhaustion too. I held him that way for another minute, deciding what to do with my monster of a boss.

And that minute was just enough time for Graves to transition back. Back from the slobbering, eager, walking dead character that had been raging just moments ago. Back to the in-control, dominant and elegant sophisticate, the part-time human. As he relaxed and stopped fighting my position, trying now to return to a full standing position and to his dignity, I knew Mortimer Graves was returning. Coming back to his role of the Zombie Billionaire.

The weird old rich guy in front of me knew how to make an effective antidote, I'll say that much. It took less than two minutes for the potent solution to have an effect, to stop the zombie regression. Lucky for me. And for Helmut.

Lucky for Graves too. His sword was on the floor, and I wouldn't have let him pick it back up. The machete may have been destroyed by Graves' sword, but the pole itself hadn't been. I'd never used a 9-foot club in the past, but I knew I could get creative. Learning on Graves' zombie skull for starters. Your narrator here is not receptive to the option of being infected by zombie spittle, nor to being munched on. Sorry Graves. In a fight to the death, your lawn care guy, Trick, would be the one walking away if he could help it.

But killing Graves wouldn't be needed, as it turned out.

"I've suddenly lost my appetite for blood, young sir. I think I'm ready about now for a plate of seasoned noodles. For dessert I'll have a dandelion salad," Graves said with a grunt, while I continued pressing him to the wall, the sharp needle still stabbing into his backside.

"It'll be fine at this point, young sir, to release me," Graves said. Followed by a gasp of pain, and an exhalation of exhaustion.

I said nothing, keeping a strong stance, the pole in a secure position, the hypodermic still thrust into Graves' butt.

"I assume you're aware, that in more ways than one, I've just had a very unpleasant experience," Graves said.

"As did I."

"But mine was a particular jolt. Something I'm not used to. I've not only had my ass kicked, but I've also had it stabbed. Please release me," Graves said.

I held him there, not certain what to do.

"Does this sound like the ramblings of a hungry zombie to you?" Graves said.

I didn't respond, although it was sounding like the

actual Mortimer Graves at that point. I held him, nevertheless.

"Kittrick Chasseur, withdraw that needle from my flesh. This instant. That's not a request."

Yep, Graves was back. I withdrew the hypodermic needle, stepped back, and stood at ease.

17

Technically, Graves wasn't all the way back yet, but the monster part of him was gone. He was trying to straighten his suit coat, then his tie, then the coat once more. Not sure what to do with himself. His eyes, looking more normal by the second, had the start of tears in them. At least you could see the pupils again.

"I...took a couple of hits to my jacket here," he said, gesturing to two tiny holes on the suit coat. One in the belly area, one to the left side of his ribcage. Slight rings of neon red blood surrounded the holes, but any bleeding had promptly stopped.

"Superficial?"

"For me, yes. An extra shot of that strong medicine, and I'll be well on my way to healing."

I said nothing, looking at Helmut, who was still confused and ready to run away. Then I glanced over to the locked door of the mansion.

"The blood from Culp out in the courtyard, when Helmut bit into him...that started the yearnings," Graves said. "The progression."

"Unlock the front door, Mortimer," I said.

"Trick, please understand. There just wasn't enough time. You and your partners got the organic material to me as quickly as you could. But I couldn't get the process completed before the transition started," Graves said. "The lichen is in the test tubes, fermenting as we speak. Next I'll put the petroleum distillate into the mixer, so the medicine can–"

"I trust you know how to formulate the antidote, Mortimer," I said. "But I gotta get back out there. Now."

"Yes, you do," Graves said.

"My gun's lying out in the courtyard. No chance you have a firearm in the house, I'm assuming."

"No. Never have," Graves said.

"Any ideas? I could get gunned down the second I step out there."

"Uh, no. Don't think that will happen. Before I came for you, I watched things on the security camera. The other one, the scumbag named Clifton, he's been taken out."

"Dead?"

"No, but he's down. Bleeding, crippled, the works. At the time, I was well into transitioning, and I must say, the scene looked tempting."

"What do you mean?" I asked.

"Clifton would have been appetizing at the time, especially considering his hostility to me recently. A revenge feast," Graves said.

I was trying to fit all of this together, the gunshots, with one lady friend seen running away when Culp forced us into the mansion. The other nowhere to be seen. Now Graves said Clifton was down. I said nothing, looking only at him, waiting.

"Then I realized," Graves continued, "with the use of one of my inside cameras, that you and Mr. Culp, and Helmut of course, had all conveniently come to me. Prey in much closer proximity than the bleeding and struggling Clifton. So I forgot him for the present time."

"Well, needless to say, things have changed. I better get out there and finish what's been started," I said. "Please open it up, Mortimer."

Who'd put Clifton out of action? Margo? Of the two women, she was closer to being a warrior. Margo was my bet. I started to lurch away, heading to the door, to escape to the courtyard and the field beyond. To find out what happened, straighten things out. To rescue. To kill if need be.

"Brace yourself, young sir," Graves said then. "Ms. Ruby is down as well. Shot. I saw when the bullet struck her."

As he said it, I could feel the air exit my lungs, my throat constrict, my head swim.

"What?"

"A bad hit, in layman's terms," Graves said.

Bad hit. Horror crashed down on me then; it felt even greater than the horror I'd just encountered with the freak now standing in front of me.

"It didn't look too promising," said Graves. He fixed his stare on me. As if to help me understand. And even with the uncharacteristically rumpled suit, his bowtie askew from the scuffle, the weary look of an old man just finished with a battle, I could see in his eyes something that was disheartening. Frightening even. The look was something I'd never seen Graves convey before.

It was sympathy.

I then knew what I was about to find out there. Graves lifted the remote, clicked it. The mechanisms shuffling within the door could be heard as it unlocked.

"Tell me, and I want the truth, Mortimer," I said. "I know it's top secret, but I don't care right now. What do you have as far as medical technology back in your lab? What kind of life-saving devices?"

"Equipment and techniques beyond my penicillin substitute?"

"Yeah."

"None. I generally just keep my fingers crossed," Graves said.

Ohhh. I dropped the pole, ran to the door, swung it open, and fled from the mansion without another word.

***

Ruby's worries were over. She laid on her back, unmoving, eyes open, as if viewing the sky. Unseeing. One leg was bent and caught under the other, the way it was when she'd fallen. When she'd died.

Ruby's right arm was over her head, the other was in Margo's lap. Margo held Ruby's still hand in both of hers. Margo was sitting next to her partner's body, tears streaming down her face, that face looking helpless. Stunned. She looked up at me as I approached, then back down at Ruby.

I took a knee next to the women, encircling Margo's shoulder with my arm. I looked out to the field, where Kevin Clifton stumbled a few steps, clearly in agony, moving away from us to the swamp, a massive patch of blood on his light blue denim shirt. On the right side of his lower back. Where he'd been shot. I watched as he fell over like a rag doll. He struggled to get back up, but couldn't.

I kissed Margo's head, and hugged her tight. I wanted to nurture her, along with myself, process the shock, but I had to get the big picture here.

"You put that punk over there in the field out of action, looks like," I whispered to her.

"I didn't shoot him. I blasted my last shots off as I scrambled away," Margo said. "It was all so fast. I was out of shells, tried to hide by the thicket over there. But Clifton was on me, got close, taking aim. Then she put him down."

She?

"Ruby shot him?" I still held her, talking softly. Margo nodded her head.

"After she'd been hit?" I asked.

"Yeah. Clifton had been straight behind her, got her

almost point black. Culp was focusing on you, I guess. I started shooting and running, I can't remember it all. But I was crouched down, and there he was in two seconds," Margo said. "He was coming in as if to finish me off, all smiles and chuckles. Over his shoulder I could see Ruby rise up, getting back to her feet."

She got off her last shot while dying. Saving Margo. Probably me too, when considering the whole scenario.

"She steadied herself and fired. It came out through his belly, Trick."

No wonder Clifton was so messed up. Not only was his lower back on the right side destroyed, but Ruby's bullet probably caught some intestinal parts too. The scumbag was finished. But I decided to speed his demise anyway.

I continued to hold Margo, but pulled her in closer, making her eyes face into my chest. So she wouldn't be able to watch. With my other hand I reached over and gently closed Ruby's eyes. I held them closed until they stayed shut on their own. Then I moved her arm from overhead to a place resting next to her body, and moved her twisted leg from underneath the other one, which had been trapping it.

We stayed that way for four or five minutes, Margo's crying coming back once, then trailing off to a drained murmur. Head down. I watched Clifton almost get back up, then fall over for the third time.

I kissed Margo's head once again. Then I gradually moved from her side, to standing. I held the butt of my recovered shotgun out to her.

"Hold this," I said. Her face was dazed, but she knew the switch had to be made from mourning to defense at any time in the current reality.

"Two shells in there, if something comes up." Then I moved away, striding back to the mansion.

18

"I'll take you up on that offer of a sword," I said to Mortimer Graves. His improvement had quickened, to say the least.

Graves didn't respond at first. Ruminating. Processing the situation.

"I see," Graves finally said, issuing a curt nod, then spinning on his heel and stepping to a massive pair of shiny wooden doors a few feet down the hall.

I waited with Helmut, the dog now nuzzling my hand. Looked like the big boy wanted me to take him with. Sorry fella, gotta run. South. Way, way south.

After I finish a certain task.

Graves was back in a few moments.

"He'll adjust," Graves said, looking at Helmut. "The poor dog has, unfortunately, witnessed my struggles against transition a time or two before this. Never as bad as today, but…"

I waited. Graves braced himself, as if in front of a full auditorium. About to make a grandiose presentation. He began.

"Mr. Kittrick Chasseur, I bequeath to you, with great pride and pleasure, an heirloom which has been in the Graves family for over 200 years."

Even with his wealth, his castle, and all that had just happened, he made a great show of his sacrifice, the giving away of the weapon a substantial loss, done with great effort. Emotional strain reflected in his once again partly handsome – but still significantly haunting – countenance. He made sure to look like he was wincing. At the loss of one sword.

Nice acting there, Graves, I thought. The Zombie Billionaire miser had at least 12 more of them. Let's speed things up here, buddy. I thought that too, didn't say it.

"Of all of the blades in my collection, this specimen will be the most suitable for you. Based on your hand size, height, and arm length."

I waited.

"That sword has been deemed 'Charlemagne.' Charlemagne came to power around 770 AD, and was mighty and greatly feared. A conqueror, a warrior. He overwhelmed the violent Saxon tribes in his region. No easy task. Charlemagne also turned the tables on many Danish pirates, which was a big industry for Denmark back then. He was a heinous murderer as far as both groups were concerned. But...he won."

Graves held out the sword, firmly encased in its leather-covered scabbard. I took it, gently, but I felt some kind of power coming from it, transferring into my body, my tissues. Possibly. Maybe it was psychological, who knows. But it gave me comfort. In an instant, I felt ready to use the ancient weapon. I clutched it tighter then, as if to protect it. As far as I was concerned, it was mine now.

And quite a step up from a pole pruner with a $16 machete attached to the end of it. I undid my belt a bit, slid the big sword sheath onto the leather, and buckled back up.

My lack of gratefulness from a moment ago was fading; if Graves had named this after the Charlemagne character, and Charlemagne was truly as Graves described, then, well...maybe there was something to this heavy, ancient blade.

But I couldn't help toggling into my impatient young prick persona just then, the embodiment of a man on a mission. Which I was. And an urgent, vile task awaited me.

"Yes, it's an heirloom. A masterpiece. I'm happy about all that, but I really couldn't care about the specifics right now, Mortimer. I just need a weapon, a big blade being ideal. You know what I'm going to use the sword for," I said.

"I certainly do."

"I'm not going to baby this thing, sir. First thing the sword will serve as is a messenger of death. As a tool of revenge. Just so you understand."

"As it should be," Graves said. "After all, it's a cutlass. That's what it exists for."

He stood there, stoic, without emotion, partly handsome, partly revolting, kind of otherworldly. I could tell he'd ended discussion on the matter.

I nodded to Graves, then extended my hand to shake his.

"Don't touch me," Graves said.

I looked into his eyes, their restored liquid blue staring back at me, at the same time hideous and hypnotizing.

"You now have some cleanup to do. As do I. Then I need to rest as soon as possible, with what I've been through," Graves said. I was about to turn away; I stopped as he again addressed me.

"Young Kittrick…"

"No need to be so formal. Trick will do."

"Ah, yes. Young Trick." His voice lowered; kind of like I imagined he did back in the old days, when some business deal had gone bad. Or when they had to break bad news to a loved and trusted employee.

"Your subcontractor, Miss Ruby…"

"My friend. My partner. My loved one," I said. He paused, looking like he was waiting out my rambling. He could perhaps no longer conceive of such things as love and friendship.

"Regarding the burial. The Minnow Man can do it," Graves said.

"Forget about it," I said.

"It would be more expeditious to do so," Graves replied. "You could be on your way, and…"

"Her burial is not just some task to mark off the checklist, Graves. It's a way to say goodbye."

"Understood." Some emotion appeared then in his mysterious eyes. Yep, there was a little human left there. "Bidding adieu. Always touchy. But doing it the right way is always important. And I haven't said it yet, but I must. I owe you my life," Graves said.

I gave him a partial bow, not daring to say a thing. But I appreciated his comment. Something was welling up in my throat, something forbidden. Wetness in my eyes. He saw it, his partly zombie eyes lighting up with recognition. With compassion, maybe. I glanced away.

"Very well. By the time you're done, I'll have the food products out for you, right at the front gate. Plus an extra 2-liter jug of fuel. I'd supply you with more, but…"

"I appreciate the extra fuel. Many thanks, Mortimer. Well, need to move out," I said, "See you next spring."

But I stood there, gripping the sword. Not leaving for some reason. Waiting for the go ahead, I guess.

"Stop stalling, Young Trick," Graves said.

I slid the sword from the scabbard, feeling its intoxicating magic, understanding for the first time perhaps what it was about these things that entranced Graves so.

"Slice him up. Like a tube of pepperoni," I said to Mortimer Graves.

"There's my boy," he replied.

***

Graves didn't say another word, instead turning on his heel, leaving. His abrupt departure was not viewed as rude. It was, in fact, a gesture I'd experienced over and over from the Zombie Billionaire. Departure, Mortimer Graves style. Quick and quiet, with an air of importance. Other things to do, it said. Get on with it.

I walked out of the Graves Mansion, toward the weedy field, shiny sword secured again in the scabbard on my belt. Toward Ruby's murderer. It was time to kill. To carry out my first execution with my new weapon, with the sword that had been given a name.

Name? I thought for a second. Uh, what had Graves called it? Chartreuse? No, Charlemagne. Yeah, that was it, Charlemagne. A conqueror, a warrior, a murderer in the eyes of his opposition.

But he won, didn't he?

One swish, and the deadly blade was once again unsheathed. I held the sword up, letting it catch a glint of sun, the blade surrounded by the backdrop of greenery, of a blue sky, fragrant breezes out of the northwest. Pastoral. In stark contrast to the scene behind me. Where one of my loved ones was on her knees weeping. And the other one lay in front of her, dead.

I whipped the sword right, then left, two practice swipes, the gentle whistle of its passage through fresh air like a subdued whisper of death. Charlemagne indeed.

The killer of Ruby, of my love, was out in the field in front of me. Wounded, and for your narrator, Mr. Trick, easy pickins. I don't have a mean streak. Not usually, anyway. This was an exception. At this point, you, the reader, can expect more blood.

***

What's there to say about the fate of Clifton? With her last act of defiance, Ruby had planted a deer rifle slug in his lower back. He couldn't run. He could barely crawl. No match for most any opponent, much less your hyper-violent narrator. No match even if I was unarmed, much less with this three-foot long sword in my grip, with its edge shaving sharp.

I approached the degenerate without a word. He pleaded, singing the blues. Not his fault, he said. He was desperate, he continued. On and on. I raised the sharp blade for the first slice.

Clifton had extended a hand to ward off the attack, as he continued the pleading. The groveling. The whining.

I cut the hand off.

As he reared back, screaming to the heavens, I toggled back into my original character. The emotions. Feeling sympathy. Yeah, old Trick Chasseur has some of that left.

Clifton kicked at me, struggling through the weeds on his back. Pathetic, helpless. I thought of walking away.

Then I pictured Ruby lying behind us, a .22 bullet through her back, probably penetrating her heart, or making a wound somewhere close to it. A wound inflicted by this piece of shit Clifton. Murder of an innocent. Ruby was their fellow human, probably one of the few left on earth. And they murdered her for what? Some extra noodles? A bag of seeds? The last little bottles of wine?

Clifton and Culp were in on it together. One was dead. This one here was next.

Clifton continued to kick at me as I walked toward him. This one's for Ruby, bitch. I whipped the glimmering blade through the air with more force than necessary.

Off came his right foot. He screamed. Then off came his left arm, just after he flipped to his belly, trying to crawl away. That one was for Margo, for the loss of her close friend, her compatriot. For an emotional wound she'd most likely never recover from. I knew I wouldn't.

He moaned, then yelled, then screamed. Keep screaming, scumbag. Once more with feeling, you piece of filth. For two more seconds. OK, time to end it.

I stabbed the cutlass down into the base of his head, through bone, into his braincase. He twitched, then lay still. All thoughts of his scheming, his backstabbing, of killing people for a serving of extra noodles, and for abducting women and using them as playthings, now gone from his mind. Along with his life force. Dissipating into the universe.

Rot in hell, I thought. You just downgraded my life; it's the least I could do in return, Clifton. Good riddance, fucker.

I let his warm corpse lie there, and marched over to where Ruby was sprawled out. Margo kneeled next to her, looking down, the crying dissipating, a sagging hopelessness seeming to overwhelm her.

***

"Wait over there," I said to Margo. "Face the mansion. Look over to the roses. Rest up. You'll need it."

"No, Trick. She was everything to me. We…"

"I said rest up," I continued. "You're going to be operating a motorcycle later today, my dear. Stay calm and rest. Sleep for a bit if you can."

"But…"

I pulled her in, gave her neck a brief caress, hugged her, issued a squeeze to her solid, slim shoulders, then let my hug wander to the center of her lean back. I let my breath channel past the soft hair by her ear. I got in close as I wanted to comfort her, but I also did it so she couldn't see the mist forming again in my eyes. The misty eye thing, that was my own private world. I waited a while until it cleared, then leaned back. We stared into each other's eyes.

"I don't want you to see the burial," I said.

She opened her mouth, but didn't say anything. Her eyes soaring wildly, desperately.

"Rest, power down for a bit, and don't watch. Look at the roses next to the mansion."

I turned away from Margo, and took my first steps toward a task that tried my soul like nothing before it.

To my relief, the Minnow Man appeared from the west, slithering from out of the swamp. A rusty shovel dangled from his hand. That tool would be particularly helpful, since more or less I had only my hands for digging. The Minnow Man looked contrite, a tiny bit of sorrow fixed on his face. He never really knew Ruby; it was respect for me and my other woman nonetheless, at least in my mind.

"I can help you carry the fallen one," the Minnow Man said.

"I've got her. You tote the shovel, I'll carry my partner," I said.

Silence intruded for fifteen seconds.

I looked at the other man, absolutely astounded I had someone else to share in this task. To help me with the ordeal, the makeshift service and burial. I couldn't, and wouldn't, subject Margo to it.

"I don't have the words," the Minnow Man said.

"But you have the shovel. Right now nothing could

be more important," I said.

The Minnow Man gave a fraction of a nod, and reached out a fist to me. We touched knuckles, he flipped the shovel over his shoulder, and I lifted Ruby's body into my arms.

19

"Who's next? Us? We'll never get her back," Margo sobbed. She was coming undone. "What are we going to do? Trick? Are you listening?"

The burial was done, and the Minnow Man had vanished back into the swamp. I looked to the green empty field, expanding before the dark, empty swamp. Abandoned neighborhoods in all directions, places once bustling with life. Now empty. Like the empty world all around us. The empty present. My soul emptying too, with Ruby snuffed out so suddenly, no longer among the living. Knowing the same could happen to the two of us, Margo and me, at almost any time. Margo's spirit was draining out. For a moment, I too was becoming drained.

All the shit that makes me who I am seeming to melt. So easy to collapse, to give in, to surrender. Stop fighting, stop running, stop groveling for food. Stop living. Take my Derringer pistol out of my pack and use it. Like with Ruby, all of my worries would be over.

Surrender would be so easy.

Then my gaze wandered to the tops of the trees on the swamp's edge, then to the ones in the swamp's interior; they'd be so beautiful in the approaching October. Soon their pinnacles would be adorned with red, orange, and yellow blazes glowing in the sun. All of the trees now topped instead with heavenly green, for another couple of weeks anyway. Green meant life. Maybe the world was not so empty, when you looked at the trees. And smelled the September breeze. Yeah, surrender would be easy. But…there was only one problem with the surrender plan.

I was still Trick Chasseur.

"What are we going to do?" Margo said again.

I looked away from the beauty of the trees.

"I'll tell you what we're gonna do," I said. "We're gonna roll out, like before, to warmer climes. Texas, just like before. To regroup, to prepare for next season up here. To rest, to eat, and to make love." She raised her eyes, locked on mine, fear still there, but fading a little. As for me, the tears which had just been welling up behind my eyes seemed to recede a little.

"Just…" Margo stammered. Her fear returning a little.

"Yeah, *just*. Just get your ass on the back of this bike."

Through the near-hysteria, she managed some exasperation. Vintage Margo. She pointed in a weak gesture at the barn, inside of which her BMW waited. "My motorcycle. We can't just leave it. We need…"

"Please shut up. We're not riding in a caravan. Get on."

"What'll happen to the bike?"

"It'll be our spare next spring. If someone breaks in and steals it, it'll be their luckiest day since the Apocalypse," I said. To soften the blow, I winked at her. The fear receded from her eyes for a moment. She looked over to where her beloved BMW was housed.

She thought about it one last time, then turned to me, looking back into my eyes. I softly scooped the back of her head, planted her arrogant and beautiful mouth with a lingering kiss, doing it the way Margo always loved. My approaching tears receded completely with that. Funny how that works.

I released the liplock, and looked into her now-dazed face.

"Ruby just saved your life," I said. "And in so doing, she probably saved mine. Now she's gone, at least physically. We need to push on. All we can do is live a life that would honor hers."

Margo looked back at me, her eyes moist. I could tell mine were too.

I gestured with a thumb to the spot behind me on the Kawasaki's seat.

"On."

***

I could smell the fragrance of her skin, her hair. We no longer had stuff like those old commercial products on hand, but we had simple organic soap, which smelled as good as any of that artificial stuff from the past. Besides, the natural smells of the human body can be pretty awesome, all by themselves. I drank in the scents wafting off Margo's body as the cycle picked up speed.

Destination: south, for now. To greater bounties, to more food. To more warm sun, to our known havens for rest. To plenty of extra loving, in hopes of repopulating this spent, contaminated land just a little.

Crass, so soon after Ruby? Depends. Could be looked at as part of our mourning, an essential ingredient in starting back up. No sense fighting it. We sped forward, down past the suburbia of yesteryear, around the bend of the aging, abandoned city they used to call Minneapolis. Continuing on the old concrete ribbon, its surface at this point growing less and less crowded with trash.

But still dodging detritus. The same old wrecks as last year, an occasional dried up body, a few cars, two pickup trucks, an abandoned semi truck. I used them as an obstacle course. Abandoned cars, ruined machines, evaporated dreams, the very human beings formerly in control of those things now themselves long decayed away.

Forced to see all that, but we continued on. For a better tomorrow, a rejuvenation and healing of this earth, a healing of whatever society remains. And to love each other…for escape, comfort, safety, and to quench our lust, for sure, but also in the hopes of continuing humankind. Through thick and thin, through safety and danger, through cold and heat, thirst and hunger. All that, and we – just two of us now – continue. Still grasping onto life.

And like I said, I'm still Trick Chasseur. Still feeling lucky to be alive.

Cool wind blasted into us from the northwest, heavy with the smells of approaching autumn chill. My lover clutched me around the midsection, her warm breath on my neck. We sped on. Directly in our path lay an old tire, and as we approached, a dented up metal trash can rolled into the lane. I slowed, skirted the debris on the road, then drifted back on course to a clear freeway, speeding back up.

Margo and I had lost a person we deeply loved. Because of evil, because of distraction, because of inopportune circumstances. But most of all, because of me. It wasn't due to bad luck. I hadn't tied up loose ends when I could have. I'd still been relying on my humanity, letting our enemies walk. Never again, I then told myself, and I haven't allowed such vulnerability since. Not once. No more loose ends. Especially the kind that will shoot you in the back. One of life's hard, hard lessons.

Further ahead of us, I could see the bedraggled figure of a zombie on the highway, lurching and jerking his way toward the center of the freeway. Apparently motivated by a food opportunity, after seeing us approaching.

There was no need for a battle. I'd give it the slip; had done it before, and it had always worked.

I slowed slightly, went over to the left lane. Formerly the fast lane. Current day zombies don't know the difference: they never yield to faster traffic. The zombie figure ahead kept going, maneuvering over until it was fully in the left lane. Prepared to intercept its lunch. I continued the motion of the cycle straight toward it, until we were only about 15 yards from colliding. The zombie reached out toward us, straining for the moving machine with the two edible lumps of flesh riding on it. Mouth agape.

I simply steered back into the right lane, the zombie unable to follow the motion. Flailing arms, twisting legs, the deteriorated body falling sideways to the filthy concrete. Its jaws still working, popping, grinding. Snapping. Like an undead crocodile.

"Later, alligator," I said, giving the cycle a burst of gas, the force of igniting nitroglycerine in the fuel making the bike vibrate. Making it fly forward like a rocket.

We accelerated ahead, uninterrupted. Then I sped up some more, feeling the beast underneath me quaking with its enthusiasm for the road. Can't get tripped up by the small stuff; someone's depending on us.

A very wealthy man, a human being always on the edge of transition to the inhuman, to the side of the undead. He'd have trouble making it without us. So we'd be back, once the snow was gone. Back to where Ruby now rested in peace, to pay her our respects. Back to the land of green, the land of plenty. To the region of my homeland. To our job, to food and shelter. To the lair of the Zombie Billionaire.

And in the meantime, as for any zombie attackers? I'll handle it. I've got a plan; it's simple, and it's the same as the plan for human attackers.

We win, they lose.

Yep, still feeling lucky to be alive. Will I continue to feel lucky?

Yeah. Because if luck evades me, I'll make my own. Count on it.

###

P. J. Hafner is a St. Paul, Minnesota, native. Both an angler and bow hunter, he also spent 15 years as a wrestler and judo fighter, and is a repeat participant in the Twin Cities marathon and other running races. He's hiked in the Blue Ridge, Cascade, Chuckanut and Rocky Mountains, as well as in Switzerland and Iceland. Hafner holds degrees in English and Kinesiology.

He is also the author of *Stalk*, *Chuckanut Stalk*, *Marathon Stalk*, *Feast of the Badger*, *Red Fang* and *Sasquatch Spectre*.